CALIFORNIA

2020

Zachary Roberts

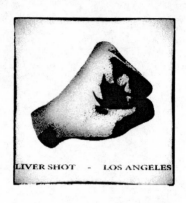

LIVER SHOT - LOS ANGELES

Published by Liver Shot Publishing
www.livershotpublishing.com

This is a work of fiction.

Library of Congress Control Number: 2017903946

CIP data available

ISBN 978-0-692-85875-2

First Edition

Published March, 2017

Edited, Designed, Photographed by Zachary Roberts

DEDICATED TO MY MOTHER AND FATHER

There are three classes of people.

Those who see,

Those who see when they are shown,

Those who do not see.

- Leonardo Da Vinci

I
Ocean

Half a dream held loosely in the front of your head is wiped to dust by the piercing echo of an electronic bell.

An exasperated groan evolves into a string of your favorite curse words, more of a declarative statement than question.

The familiarity of the white light illuminating your bedroom provides an abrupt reality check. You reach for the phone.

EMERGENCY ALERT
October 1, 2020 3:15 A.M.
TSUNAMI WARNING FOR SOUTHERN CALIFORNIA
8.6 magnitude earthquake 200 miles off the coast of Los Angeles
EVACUATE IMMEDIATELY
Tsunami waves up to 30 feet expected
San Louis Obispo: 3:39 a.m.
Santa Barbara: 3:43 a.m.
Los Angeles: 3:51 a.m.
San Diego: 4:04 a.m.

Confusion gives way to stomach knots. You quickly flip the bedroom and living room lights, which work to your brief relief, then turn the TV to a broadcast channel. Jessica Winchester is wearing a smart red blazer and practicing proper inhalation before speaking when the Emergency Broadcast System hijacks the airwaves.

The awful screech of the Emergency Broadcast digital header repeats three times as text relays "This Broadcast Station or Cable System Issued a Tsunami Warning."

A monotone human delivers the message.

"The National Weather Service has issued a Tsunami Warning for the coastal areas of Southern California, including the following counties: San Louis Obispo, Santa Barbara, Ventura, Los Angeles, San Diego. This is a result of an 8.9 earthquake off the coast of Los Angeles that struck at 3:15 in the morning. The tsunami warning means a tsunami is imminent, and the coastal locations in the warned areas need to self-evacuate immediately. Tsunami waves of thirty feet are expected."

You are standing barefoot in your pajamas on the second floor of a one bedroom apartment on Pacific Ave in Venice, California. The pavement outside is thirteen feet above sea level, and your front door is less than five hundred feet from the alluring sands of Venice Beach. The expletives flow freely as you franticly plan your "self-evacuation."

The pooling adrenaline brought forth by imminent crisis tunnels your focus. These are quick, precise decisions as you dress in layers of warm clothing.

"The entire building is less than thirty feet."

Black Civilianaire jeans, black Saucony sneakers, black Patagonia fleece jacket, and a black Real Madrid snap back cap.

"I wear the black for the poor and beaten down."

Odd time for humor. Also an odd time to be unemployed and fresh off the sale of your leased crossover SUV. You look at your white Bianchi Via Nirone 7 Claris Compact road bike hanging on the hook installed in the bedroom ceiling. The Emergency Broadcast System continues to screech.

You grab your keys, wallet, and cell phone and run to the kitchen. The first responder sirens loop in the distance, and fade further into the distance. The sound of tires turning on gravel mixes with engines igniting and the stereo whoosh of cars zipping below your kitchen window. Your personal items slide into a plastic sandwich bag and you chug a full glass of water. A startling metallic crunch precedes what sounds like someone dropping an aquarium full of icicles onto asphalt concrete. The noxious odor of exhaust wafts into your kitchen, along with the sweet smell of radiator coolant, or maybe wiper fluid. Horns are blaring. People are shouting. Cars are driving on the wrong side of the street. Everyone got the message.

"How am I going to ride deep enough inland without getting my head caved in?"

Each second the bike seems less and less of an option. It is time to make a decision. Jessica Winchester cuts back in mid-sentence.

"—can be assured if they remain. If evacuation is impossible, the third floor or higher of a reinforced concrete building may offer protection, but such a building should only—"

Your eyes are wide as dinner plates while pupils dilate. Rack your brain.

An electrified mind is floating above Venice, starting from the south. The uninspired blocks of glass and steel—filing cabinets for yuppies, contemptible hipsters, and milquetoast trust fund stewards—those condominiums in the Marina are too far away. The beachfront townhouses and triple decker homes are doomed. You picture the businesses on Washington Blvd and try to remember how many floors the Cow's End coffee shop is. Is it two... is it three? You know the owner lives above the shop and might be hunkered down. The second floor balcony of the Venice Whaler is a guaranteed spot to get your ticket punched. Abbot Kinney. One and two floor restaurants. Robert Downey Jr.'s house is three floors of concrete. He seems like a man of the people, if he's in town and not off shooting *Metal Dude 9: Return of the Cube.*

You feel something spark in the center of your skull. Hotel Erwin. Six floors of concrete with a rooftop bar. Ten streets north on Pacific Ave. Your sneakers pivot and you take that explosive first step towards the front door. The TV warbles as you instinctively lock the knob while pulling the door shut. No sign of your neighbors as you take eleven stairs in three steps and bust through the building exit onto Pacific Ave.

The northbound lane of Pacific Ave is blocked by a smashed out dinosaur of a black rust colorated Mitsubishi pickup. Northbound drivers have completely commandeered the southbound lane as they swerve around the seeping carcass of Japanese engineering. Eighty yards to the north, Pacific Ave intersects with one-way eastbound South Venice Blvd. Gridlock is forming as cars from the north, south, and west jockey for position on one of the major east-west thoroughfares of Los Angeles.

Since 1932, California State Route 187 stretches from the sea through the Interstate 10 and 110 interchange downtown. More than enough runway to escape anything Poseidon can conjure. As you hasten your pace on the sidewalk, moving north towards the intersection, a Range Rover jumps the curb seven feet in front of you. Birds of paradise explode skyward as the SUV weaves two wheels on the sidewalk and two wheels on the avenue, scraping against shrubbery and freshly graffitied wooden fencing.

"~~WSP PBGK MFK~~ IF YOU AIN'T VSLC GO HOME
FAR WEST VSLC2X 5th 6th 7th"

The SUV swerves and dips off the corner curb, tires chirping and spinning out of synch but successfully jumping the queue eastward on South Venice Blvd.

A persistent and biting chill confirms 4 a.m. is usually the coldest moment of any twenty-four hour spin of the globe.

Lingering moisture adds a hazy glow to the streetlights, but you can see deep enough into the black night to make out the next intersection. Separated from South Venice Blvd by a city owned parking lot and occasionally proposed site for homeless housing, North Venice Blvd is the one-way westbound portion of Venice Blvd. Beginning at noon every weekend between March and December, a slow moving tourist caravan of rattling subwoofers and crammed coolers creeps westward on North Venice Blvd; they part ways with a small fortune to park their metallic steeds, get tuned up in the bone warming rays of sunshine, and come dusk inch their way towards South Venice Blvd and the eastern road back to reality. This too often witnessed phenomenon dances across your mind's eye as you contrast that image with a plangent Ford Mustang tearing off from the pack and roaring its throaty dual exhaust the wrong way down one-way North Venice Blvd. Streetlights bounce a shine off the midnight blue paint job, and you notice the black rims from the gleam provided by an aqua underbody LED light system. Another car follows before double barreled bedlam is pointing eastward at every option. This is no place for pedestrians.

Pacific Ave is the westernmost scar civilization has carved into the Venice coastline. Beside the homes and apartments on Pacific Ave is a wide alley named Speedway that extends north all the way to Santa Monica. The quintessential west Los Angeles alleyway, consisting of a single wide lane indented to collect stormwater and bookended by trash bins and two story apartment buildings crawling with wires and old satellite dishes left behind by the revolving door of tenants that had to tuck tail back to wherever "home" was.

West of Speedway are the beachfront triple decker jumbo mortgages and overleveraged townhouses, and then land becomes sea at your very own edge of the world. You decide Speedway gives you the higher probability of avoiding a one sided street fight with a turbocharged V8 four wheel drive that has seen nothing but city streets and is just itching to throw some weight around. It feels like the most realistic, high-stakes video game as you pick your moments and stutter step through the erratic autos to scamper west on Virginia Ct. and then north onto Speedway.

As you dodge traffic at Speedway and South Venice Blvd a six floor apartment building towers over the beach. Most of the lights are on. A woman is peering off one of the south facing balconies. Midstride you think for a moment whether or not you could talk your way into one of these high floor apartments. The building appears to be constructed of cinderblocks and brick, and as you look directly to your left at the dimly lit beach you decide this building does not qualify as reinforced concrete. Speedway traffic becomes one-way southbound as you cross Venice Blvd and sprint north past 20th Ave. The little streets are flying by, Hotel Erwin is not far off. The alley provides ample space to run as the single line of vehicles is barely moving due to three automated cars failing to compute the correct method to handle this unique emergency situation. The human drivers have no room to circumvent these zero emission early adopters.

You sprint by a metal cage fabricated to secure the industrial dumpster guarded within. Across the cage "Venice" and

"Muscle Beach" are spray-painted in a stylized blue font over a sunset red and orange background. On the building façade is a two story mural of *Pumping Iron* era Arnold Schwarzenegger flexing his signature Gold's Gym power pose. Since 1991, the north side of the same building is plastered with a "young lion" era Jim Morrison, slinking shirtless in leather pants, mic in hand. You've watched the surrounding surface of the building go from chipped white paint, to blue, to the current sunset red, but in a rare instance of gentrified respect no owner will paint over a Venice mural by Rip Cronk.

With cars approaching a standstill people are beginning to legitimately lose their minds. Frenzied Venetians are running in every direction but west. The crackheads and meth smokers that only begin to flirt with the idea of winding down around 5 a.m. are now piling their belongings into the centers of large blue tarps, muttering and screaming the secret languages only they decipher. One of the ubiquitous white guys with long blonde dreads is wearing an M-65 field jacket and jolting his clenched fists in and out of a folded arm position, his grinding teeth half suppressing some kind of stressed chant as he sporadically darts about in a demented moshing dance. His black brethren are collecting bedding, clothing, bicycle frames, and various arts and crafts. Some have already cued the jangling orchestra of shopping carts crashing across broken pavement. For a split second you feel a tinge of pride knowing you are one of the few who will have witnessed the unfathomable crackhead exodus of Venice.

A man in a track suit is running north on the boardwalk shaking a flashlight and attempting to alert people. As usual, and despite a supposed Venice Beach substation, there are no police in sight. As you pass the Morrison mural and cross 18th Ave the rooftop of Hotel Erwin comes into view.

3

Your stride shortens as you reach Speedway and 17th Ave. You've run a frenzied and surreal three tenths of a mile and your skin is radiating a pulsing heat. You feel the sweat tingling against the dense cooling mist of the ocean air. Your senses are buzzing with adrenaline and you feel the sudden need to determine how much time it took to arrive. You rifle through your pockets and the sandwich bag to check your phone. 3:32 a.m. Seventeen minutes since you were shaken from a dream to a nightmare. Seventeen minutes of mainlined testosterone, cortisol, dopamine, estrogen, and serotonin. Nineteen minutes to Armageddon.

Overlooking the world famous Ocean Front Walk promenade and planted between Speedway and Pacific Ave stands Hotel Erwin. Six stories and topped off by High Rooftop Lounge, the only rooftop bar and lounge in Venice Beach. The first floor of the building exterior is covered in ivy. You're facing the steel barrier gate for the alley entrance to the parking garage. As you examine the construction you notice it is most likely a wooden building enhanced by a stucco façade and whatever additional design magic went down during its 2012 remodel. Cursing your fuzzy memory, this does not qualify as reinforced concrete, but you're heading to the roof considering the end is extremely nigh. You book down 17th Ave towards the main entrance on Pacific Ave. As you're rounding left into the main entrance driveway you peer out onto Pacific Ave. A sea of brake lights and blaring horns fade past your field of view. You decide to take the extra ten seconds to step into the street and look north at Windward Ave, where the lit VENICE sign hangs between the iconic colonnaded buildings Abbot Kinney erected in 1905.

The Windward Ave intersection has an X shaped crosswalk allowing all four street corners to cross forward or diagonally. This entire X is blanketed with cars facing all manner of directions, rejecting any style of traffic law. You see a white Subaru facing your position with the driver side door wide open, and the passenger door snapped off a few feet away on the pavement. You notice the Subaru is empty. More people are running: all shapes, colors, and sizes, in all manner of clothing, or lack thereof, and all running east.

A Honda CBR1000RR with the Repsol paint job and aftermarket exhaust bounces one hundred and ten decibels off the Bank of Venice Public House and makes a brief appearance in the intersection, before T-boning a Ford Explorer intent on swerving around the abandoned Subaru. The motorcyclist is briefly promoted to astronaut as the bike launches him high into the air, his flailing body reaching its zenith, then falling in apparent slow motion, landing on the roof of the Mao's Kitchen restaurant on the northeast corner of the intersection. The freakishly bizarre nature of your current situation, coupled with the desensitization of a YouTube generation, has you staring mouth agape in a dreamlike state.

You notice the Subaru is not the only empty vehicle, and receive a sharp jolt back to reality when a Jeep Grand Cherokee fifteen feet in front of you unloads four desperate passengers obviously abandoning their eastward journey, fully intent on the six story building fortune has presented. Space might be limited. You pivot on your left foot and turn clockwise, eyeing the lobby entrance and once more calling on that explosive first step to scamper past the entrance and graffiti mural by Norm Will Rise.

4

You cross the threshold to be met by a crowd of panicking people packing and unpacking knickknacks in and out of backpacks and cases propped on the reception sofa. The sofa starts out sea green on the ends before changing to army green and then olive in the center of what seems to be a suede assault on your ocular muscles. Seven white Rusty brand surfboards rise up behind the sofa against a slate grey wall. To your left is the granite countered reception desk manned by a pretty Filipino girl in her early twenties. She's looking proper in a blue button down shirt and staring at you with alarmingly wide eyes and a mouth frozen open in trepidation. You bank to your right and cut through the backpack crowd. You're not waiting for permission and you know the geography, it seems a fool's anchorage to wait for the single brushed metal elevator that may or may not be in service. The Grand Cherokee gang has piled in behind you and engages the front desk agent in breathless conversation. You've turned the corner by the elevator and to your immediate elation slap down the handle on an unlocked doorway to the stairwell.

"Feet, don't fail me now."

For some reason your equilibrium has you feeling like Scooby Doo running in place at the sight of a ghost, but the projector in your brain shows sharp cut cement stairs consumed at a healthy pace. You've hit the third floor and the stairwell door is open. You see panic down the hallway, half the doors are ajar and luggage, bed sheets, and wine bottles litter the corridor. White walls and a steel railing, you're at the fourth floor. The stairwell door is open and the corridor looks similar to the third floor except there is a large bulldog of a man with both his hands in the air, fingers spread wide and emphasizing with his palms as if they were amplifying his message.

"Please stay in your rooms! You are safe in your rooms. Fill any containers with cold water. You are safe in your rooms, please stay in your rooms."

Acknowledging the pulsing veins on the tan temples of his shaved head and pinstripe suit cut two sizes too large, you assume this man is some sort of hotel security. You don't agree with the message and proceed skyward.

Your chest is burning as you continue to vault stairs. You make the conscious effort to ignore discomfort and focus your concentration on the flexing fibrous tissue that will put you in the best position for security and well-being. Launching your metatarsals off what must be close to the final set of steps, the signature twin-faced sheepskin of a chestnut pair of Ugg boots enters your sightline, and you have to reach out with both hands and grab railing to prevent your face from colliding with one of the more impressively wide, bubbly, heart shaped and yoga draped derrières in the 90291 zip code. A sharp featured blonde girl with a long tight braid briefly points her hazel gaze at you, and you notice the same fear and desperation that you've seen in every pair of eyes locked in the last twenty minutes. She turns frontward and you are looking beyond her at a rather tightly pressed crowd of people squeezing through the single door leading to the rooftop lounge. You feel fortunate to be proceeding at all as you take each remaining step slowly and deliberately with the group. There is a murmuring prattle, but most in the stairwell are silently striving towards the doorway to salvation. You've progressed to the final flight of stairs and listen to the clamor of the assembly on the roof. A lumbering, scraping echo reverberates up the stairwell like someone just dumped four sacks of potatoes down a trash chute. You hear that signature east coast bellow of the night watchman, but can't determine if syntax was involved, or what message was delivered.

You know from prior inebriated tangential conversations with wait staff and DJs that the hotel has one hundred twenty-two rooms, and since 2017 the maximum occupancy of the rooftop lounge is one hundred forty-eight people. The roof is noticeably more packed at this moment than any given midnight. The rooftop deck is roughly eighty feet wide and over three hundred feet long. The stairs and elevator lead out onto a forty foot walkway that guides to the remaining lounge section of the deck. The walkway is enclosed by a steel railing with glass walls and spreads into an elongated rectangle that surrounds a roof structure. The outer edges of the rectangle are divided into a series of chic mini lounges that feel like a collection of VIP booths on a rectangular runway. Each lounge area feels isolated as one side boasts spectacular ocean and city views, and the other side is a railed off walkway surrounding the roof structure. If your friends were in the section on the opposite side of the deck you would have to do a lap around the walkway to get to them.

In any other situation the strategically placed umbrellas and drought conscious foliage, the grey paneled flooring, comfortable L shaped furniture, polished steel and glass partitions might soothe the soul. The foreboding shiver of ominous dread is universally palpable. As consolation the elegant silver Thermo Tiki Deluxe propane pyramid style heat lamps are all displaying their dancing flame. Despite the monumental anxiety, part of you is proud of your current position and choice. This seems like the best possible venue. The deck is well beyond capacity, yet there is just enough mobility that you as one person are able to meander your way down the walkway and past the DJ booth en route to the north or southwest corner.

As you maneuver towards your destination the walkway's glass partition rattles to the heavy slam of an industrial door. You turn to see the security guard facing the walkway with his back to the stairwell door, arms outstretched and pressed against the building. He turns and puts both emphatic palms against the door, his left knee bent forward and right leg extended like the back of a poorly tailored tripod.

"Look, it is not safe to have this many people on the deck! You are safe above the third floor. There is more than enough room on four and five. Pick a room! I cannot let you out here. Relocate to a room!"

5

You've found your way to the southwest corner, partially
separated from the walkway by a four foot high rectangular
marble planter topped with Mexican thread grass mixed
amongst assorted agave, aloe, and echeveria succulents. An
ebony rattan wicker sectional deck sofa with aqua cushions is
accompanied by two ivory cylindrical cocktail tables, for
those Smoke on the Water mezcal aperitifs. A tall Tufts blue
umbrella is reflecting the warmth of the heat lamp. You're
standing at the steel railing with your knee against the glass
overlooking the path you took to get here, Mr. Morrison, and
the entirety of the Santa Monica Bay.

Not until you absorb the expanse of this inimitable oceanic
panorama are you cognizant of the radiant silver light
bathing everything in view. You look over your shoulder and
realize tonight's lighting is courtesy of a most dramatically
full and luminous, captivating and scarred celestial body.
The perfect circle looms substantial, phosphorescence
glowing at the highest volume. If someone asked you, you
wouldn't be able to describe what you were feeling, but it
tingles your scalp, you feel it in your teeth. You think for a
second.

"The full moon brings high tide."

You turn to the coast and peer into darkness, scanning the
black horizon from Malibu to the twinkling lights of Rancho
Palos Verdes. Silver light is shimmering off puddled wet
sand further off shore than you have ever seen. The tide isn't

just low, it doesn't exist. The distinctive concrete tower serving as the Venice Beach lifeguard headquarters is on the sand to the south at 2300 Ocean Front Walk. The hexagonal observation tower has three directional spotlights swiveling concentrated light across the coast. South of the tower, thirteen hundred feet of wood and concrete extend into what should be ocean. As a spotlight crawls along the Venice Fishing Pier you see the full stretch of every piling from pier to ocean floor. The tide has retreated well beyond the length of the pier. You see how many jagged rocks dot the ocean floor surrounding the pier and reach a greater understanding as to why so many drunken late night jumpers don't return to the surface, the resulting sirens and occasional helicopter forcing you to lie in bed and stare at the ceiling.

Spotlights sporadically cast a long flickered shadow, and you realize some psychos have ambled out to experience the tide recession. You can't determine if they be vagabond, civilian, tourist, or gentrifying hipster. Surveying north from the lifeguard headquarters your gaze washes over so many locations that have been immortalized in that Southern California Los Angeles zeitgeist. The Venice Recreation Center and the benches, machines, dip and pullup bars of Muscle Beach. The speedbag stands and the handball courts. The dilapidated two story boardwalk building that used to house the Medical Kush Beach Club, when cannabis was half legal with a bribed physician's note. A discerning connoisseur could acquire an eighth of Diablo OG at the dispensary window, walk into the next room to pull up a stool at the hash bar, rip a bowl of Blue Dream hashish through frosted glass heated by a blow torch wielding hottie, and sink into a leather couch overlooking the boardwalk, palm trees swaying and glittering in the sun before the mighty Pacific. Bottle that.

The famous basketball courts are empty. Spotlights briefly throw light on the public art walls and ten foot cones that get a daily coat of sanctioned graffiti. Since 2001, Mark di Suvero's *Declaration* sculpture gracefully extends balanced and proclaiming steel arms sixty feet into the sky. You've always wondered whether the massive metal sculpture was just the letter V, a nautical instrument, or indeed a rumored Masonic symbol. The lights can't reach the skate park, but moonlight is outlining every curve and contour of the six mini pools and one large kidney shaped concrete bowl. A Z-boy's wet dream that appeared thirty-seven years after the Zephyr Team was draining pools in north Santa Monica and the San Fernando Valley.

After the exodus you witnessed earlier you're shocked to notice the amount of people and belongings strewn about the rolling knolls of grass and scuffed dirt that constitute the remainder of the promenade. A white woman who could be thirty-five or fifty-five is wearing a black bikini top and tattered jean shorts, doing an amphetamine inspired version of the running man around a heavy boombox on the boardwalk pavement. Three unidentifiable males wearing loose pants and large sweatshirts with hoods over their heads are congregated in a tight circle, skateboards in hand. A black man with braids is leaning against a concrete wall near his two person tent, shopping cart stacked to the brim with blankets, clothing, and cardboard. There is a wheelchair with multiple foam mats stacked and taped to the seat and arm rests. He is rapidly playing an empty plastic bucket with drumsticks. Some people on the west facing railing of the hotel are yelling down to them.

"Run, you kooks! There's a tsunami coming!"

No response.

Deep in the distance to the north blinks the world's only solar-powered Ferris wheel at Pacific Park on the Santa Monica Pier. The candy colored wheel towers over one hundred thirty feet. The wheel's stunning light show is in full effect: blue, red, yellow, green, white, and magenta LEDs are flashing a pattern flowing outward as the wheel spins, creating an explosive and hypnotic kaleidoscope of galvanized steel. There are no spotlights on the pier, but enough light is generated by the wheel and surrounding roller coaster that you can see the full extent of the pilings and the unsettling reality that the ocean has receded beyond the length of the pier.

The characteristic whir of a quadcopter returns your attention to Venice. Two police drones equipped with facial recognition technology are buzzing one hundred feet apart as they float westward. One of them is conducting a sweep of the Erwin roof, shifting and banking along the south edge of the roof deck. You can see the blinking green lights on two of the propeller arms. The camera swivels and reports. Very helpful. You look down at the LAPD Pacific Substation on the promenade almost directly in front of you. The structure

sits silently in darkness and a Toyota Tacoma TRD LAPD
pickup hibernates in the only occupied parking space.

You reach back into the sandwich bag. 3:47 a.m. Holding
your phone you notice most of your compatriots are
frantically tapping away at theirs. A few are holding them
landscape to document the rare occasion for their friends and
family, real and imaginary. The deep chop of news or police
helicopters reverberate across the inland vista. You make a
mental inventory of the people occupying your section of the
lounge.

6

Adriana is an undeniably beautiful twenty-seven year old with black and red hair. The flash in her brown eyes, pouty lips, and aggressively filled out jeans suggest there is significant Latin influence. She is holding an eighteen karat gold crucifix her former trust fund boyfriend bought her in Paris at the Notre Dame Cathedral gift shop. She dipped the cross in the holy water as the ten bells rang. Always a top finisher in the bikini contests back in Florida, she took her talents to Los Angeles and quickly landed a bit part as eye candy in a film you might have seen. The life was comfortable, and the road ahead seemed paved with opportunities, but they quickly dried up as she realized the most beautiful girl in every small town had the same idea she did. She retained her integrity within the industry and wouldn't sleep with an A list director or two that had invited her out to their mansions that were unfortunately perfumed by wet dogs and cigars. She maintains a sturdy daily cannabis habit and manages to get by on periodic paid modeling gigs. Expenses are contained as she is expertly and casually dating five different gentlemen that are all eager to buy her dinner. There is the infrequent donation when she joins a private jet to Las Vegas with her über rich contacts networked via bikini teams past. She is intelligent and creative, and applying none of those gifts as she frequents the happy hours of Los Angeles.

Calvin is a lifetime local, a thirty-one year old black man that grew up in a two bedroom bungalow on 6th Ave in the Oakwood section of Venice. Along with his cousin, he was a highly touted high school hoops prospect. He felt the pressure of honest expectations against the impact of his uncle, a Venice Shoreline Crips shot caller. Calvin committed to the University of Southern California when they offered an athletic scholarship; until the summer after graduation when he was in the front passenger seat of a pulled over vehicle, talking to LAPD with twenty-eight individually packaged grams of cannabis, three and a half grams of powder cocaine, and an M9 Beretta under the seat. His cousin proceeded to play ball at UCLA, with a brief stint in the NBA, and a fairly lucrative career in the Spanish ACB league. Calvin had few options but to climb the ladder in his corner of the underworld. He doesn't have to do much dirt these days, and oversees a small crew of his own. He is jovial and quick to laugh, sharp witted and equipped with his own brand of improvisationally delivered comedy, sometimes at the expense of those in the room. Behind his smile is the regret of that squandered potential, a quiet sadness for those he has harmed, and a silent yearning to do, and be, good.

Brian is a ginger with an ironic mustache. When ByteBabble bought up two blocks of Venice real estate he jumped at the opportunity to leave his job as a media buyer. Riddling his resume with lies, he was able to fast track his application through his best friend's sister, a ByteBabble human resources coordinator. It took slightly longer than planned as she kept trying to print the document through a powered off printer, but Brian was able to land his dream job and move to Brentwood in 2016. He treats Venice locals as if they were salt to his snail exterior, and moves about ByteBabble's "campus" in coworker caravans shepherded by a security detail. He doesn't have to spend much money on nightlife as there is always a sales rep from a media company taking him out for entertainment, and if it's not him specifically he can usually spy a rep in the bar entertaining someone else and tell the bartender to put his one hundred eighty dollar tab on the rep's corporate card. Yeah, that one over there. He feels good about sticking them with the tab and resents them for making two or three times as much as he does, even though a normally functioning fifth grader could do his job. He is deep in the friend zone with numerous female friends and coworkers who are intrigued by the eccentricity of his too short pastel shorts and avant-garde graffiti Polaroids. If one of these friends is not a coworker, and he is feeling frisky, he will dose them with GHB at the bar and offer to escort them home in an Uber, changing course to his apartment when she passes out. Currently he is in Venice and not at home in Brentwood because last night was the Townhouse with a sales rep, smashing Moscow mules with a cocaine chaser. He was recently banned from Uber for slapping a driver, and it was an hour wait at 2 a.m. for a yellow cab. He decided he would stumble up to ByteBabble and sleep it off in the cushy nap room, waking up around 7 a.m. to splash cold water on his face, fix his hair, and make an appearance long enough to tell his boss he was sick and heading home. He is proud all of his sick days this year have been used for hangovers. He was jolted from sleep by the alert on his phone, and quickly shuffled to the Erwin while his pores expelled vodka fumes.

Etienne and Simone met in their late twenties over €13 Heinekens while taking a break from the dance floor at a club called Amnesia on the island of Ibiza. Five years later living in Nice they welcomed little baby Lyle. A software engineer, Etienne wanted to use two of his five weeks of vacation and surprise his wife with a trip down the California coast before they spend Christmas in northern France with his parents. It is their first time in the United States, and tomorrow morning they are scheduled to pile their little family into a rental car and spend the remaining three days of their vacation in San Diego. Instead, they are bundled in sweats and jackets, huddled together in apprehension. Nine month old Lyle is in his warmest clothes and wrapped in a blanket, topped off with a black and white horizontally striped cap, his large, deep blue eyes looking straight ahead.

7

A pervasive roar drowns out the nervous pontifications of the crowd. All eyes forward. The spotlights confirm the nightmare is real. From the depths of the Pacific a torrent of foaming water sweeps towards you with complete indifference. A wave seemingly no larger than what would break on a good surf day in the Santa Monica Bay, only this wave seems to stretch from Malibu to Redondo.

The sound is entirely unnerving. The increasingly ferocious whitecapped wave is cresting at multiple sections. The amplitude appears short of thirty feet, though this does not reassure you in the least as the thundering roar is growing exponentially. Offshore the wave sounds like a derailed freight train colliding with an entire runway of afterburning jets. The hoodie clad tweakers and running man beach bunny are sprinting down 17th Ave and out of view. The man playing the bucket is now standing with his arms at his side, facing the ocean.

The wave seems frozen in time for a moment, yet somehow increasing in glassy amplitude, a glistening wall growing on approach. The wave nears the piers and suddenly a rushing tide materializes on the shore as if it was previously invisible. The tide moves at an incredible pace swallowing the beach and diffusing into the Ocean Front Walk promenade. Splashing and breaking against the smooth concrete of the Venice Skate Park pool, lurching inland in the night like a phantom levee had disintegrated. It was as if there was a secret sea underneath the hull of Venice and someone had shotgunned a massive hole in the bilge.

The salt chuck surge rockets past the LAPD Tacoma above wheel height and the chassis dips and sways. Splashing and spraying like a wave crashing into a tide pool, the rush of blue-green blackwater foam is caroming off palm trees and curbs, ricocheting into the air as it collides with the boardwalk businesses. The stoic man with the drumsticks is shin deep and appears at peace as his belongings are swept around him and carried down 17th Ave or pressed against the merchant shacks. The tide has charged beyond the hotel and everything in sight is layered with seawater.

The first wave explodes against the Venice Pier and the Santa Monica Pier simultaneously. The strength of the impact is obvious as whitewater rockets sixty feet, departed in black sky. The wave you initially discounted is caressing the cement top section of the Venice pier, which you know is twenty feet tall. You can see the ocean beyond the wave, a noticeably larger wave is not far behind, and there are more whitecaps as far back as vision allows. The sound is almost deafening, but not loud enough to completely drown out the distraught cussing of everyone on the roof. Before the wave travels the length of the Venice pier it experiences numerous closeouts, breaking along its entire length at various points. It feels as if there is a hidden demon gesticulating above the wave, inhaling all the oxygen in the atmosphere.

Buildings tremor with an explosion resonating across the bay. If there were any birds left in the trees they would scatter or plummet from the sky in cardiac arrest. Despite its distance away and below, you can feel the weight of the wave slamming against what used to be beach. More whitewater blasts high into the sky while a ferocious surge heads east at a menacing pace.

The tsunami hurtles whitewater off the concrete walls at the handball courts. The LAPD Tacoma relents to the profane power of the water, bobbing and rotating as it quickly sails east towards the boardwalk shops. It never occurred or mattered to you that these shops are fundamentally ferrous metal and plywood plopped down on the boardwalk, usually run by first generation immigrants selling amusing t-shirts, funnel cakes, Chinese sunglasses, surf and skate equipment, henna tattoos, and bicycle rentals.

That enduring dreadlocked man is completely consumed like a boulder in the path of an avalanche. The tsunami wave collides with the storefronts, immediately making short work of the façades: the storefronts are buckling and crumpling with a sound like one thousand Charbray bulls tap dancing on a hot tin roof. The lack of resistance by these structures surprises you despite their shoddy construction. The LAPD Tacoma tears through one of the businesses. Hundreds of flimsy excuses for eyewear, polarized and non, disperse into the blackwater. A concoction of sheet metal, wood, and a swirl of indistinguishable random items combine to form the sinister deluge barraging your position.

The aggressively displaced tide reaches you with a force that is even more jarring than the initial wave break on the beach.

Hotel Erwin shakes to its foundation as the tsunami and transported debris strike the west side of the building like a nuclear powered aquatic locomotive. You can taste the salt and feel the sea spray on your face as the sounds of screams and shattering windows resound from the floors below. They correspond with the screams on the roof deck. You are afraid to look over the edge, but it seems like the surge is maybe half way up the second story. These former businesses now in countless fractured pieces, stirring and spinning east as a floating caravan. The LAPD Tacoma has gyrated towards the Erwin and smashes into the west side of the building, breaking more glass and releasing a sound that was probably the parking garage gate buckling under tons of force.

White smoke billows near the tattoo shop in one of the colonnaded buildings to the north on Windward Ave. It is surreal to see so many palm trees partially submerged in an angry sea. This provides the illusion that you've discovered some new breed of pygmy palm that only grows on open water. Up Speedway, a small public parking lot has transformed into a deranged line dance of sedans and SUVs jouncing, revolving, and crumpling together. A few are breaking formation and rafting east on Windward Ave. A Nissan Rogue ends its journey prematurely by ramming into a column and wedging itself across a store window and the colonnade. You've spied more than one propane tank floating in the detritus—the light provided by streetlights and the full moon expose the beautiful bands of color indicating the presence of a chemical sheen or oily substance—red, orange, yellow, green, blue, indigo, and violet sway in the flotsam.

The screaming climbs another octave. The lifeguard spotlights are fixed west and deliver a truly heart-stopping panorama. A second tsunami wave is two hundred feet from either pier. Your stomach drops as you feel pins and needles across your forearms and upper body. You can easily see water spitting and undulating up the face of the wave as every yard between you ticks into oblivion. A slowing of time more twisted than the first pauses the image just long enough for you to absorb how much force is behind this wall of water towering over forty feet. The Venice pier duck dives into the wave. The Santa Monica pier does not eat the wave as well as its little brother, and the world famous solar powered Ferris wheel is ripped and warped from its base as if it were constructed from Popsicle sticks and not galvanized steel. For a brief moment the spokes flash out one last dance of color before turning black and ripping apart in a summersault of deadly projectiles. You think you see a few pilings spit up into the sky, but that pier is a fair clip to the north, and without the light show darkness has swallowed the view. You're not too worried about your neighbors up the coast though, every single bourgeoisie north of Wilshire Blvd is protected by bluffs clocking in at over one hundred feet tall. Waves will ricochet off the natural barrier and the condominiums, yoga studios, yogurt shops, and genuinely gorgeous Palisades Park will remain intact.

Similar to the first, the wave breaks at various points along its entire crest. It crashes into the beach like someone had sunk dump trucks full of Composition C-4 all along the coast and detonated them in unison. At this point you can't even hear the screaming. Half of your mind is deaf to the world and the other half is overwhelmed with a roar that sounds like eighty-one Superdomes filled to the brim with fans approaching a .33 blood alcohol content. The promenade is already submerged, and any structures or autos that might absorb some force have been demolished or swept away. The tower of whitewater claws towards the heavens.

From this mountainous mass springs an ominous force with little resistance along its direct path to you. A few palms bend and briefly give fight, but they either snap or the dirt they're planted in enters another dimension and they become colossal frond tipped arrows in a clumsy eastward salvo. The foundation of the sixty foot steel *Declaration* sculpture has been unearthed and the entire installation is toppling end over end at a broken tempo.

The westernmost portion of Hotel Erwin is a four story addition to the original building. Standing a full two stories short of the roof deck and remainder of the hotel, this addition seems like it was added to extend the subterranean parking garage and provide balconied rooms overlooking the ocean. As the second, obviously more significant tsunami surge rockets towards the building you can hear a rolling stampede of foot traffic on the top floor of the addition and the fifth floor of the hotel.

The tsunami throws the full force of its blackwater wave, trees, debris, and the lingering LAPD Tacoma into the side of the hotel, shaking the foundation with earthquake force. The entire roof deck is showered with whitewater as if the hotel had suddenly decided to raft a class V rapid. A sea foam tentacle reaches up and halts the propellers of one of the police drones, deading it in the black sky, momentarily motionless and paralyzed at altitude before plunging into the drink. The glass partitions and railing on the west side of the building shatter. The force of the impact has sent people off the north and south edges of the building. They ragdoll into the surging blackwater and head east down Windward Ct and 17th Ave, swinging their arms in the air counterclockwise as they try and remain buoyant during the rapid journey.

The lowest level of the hotel addition seems to deform and contort before warping wood erupts in a dramatic, splintered snapping. The entire addition completely separates from the hotel and begins to lean forward. From your vantage point you can see the main entrance portion of the rooms all the way through to the clear glass of the western balconies. In one room you see the back of a wispy blonde woman sporting a bandana and flowing apricot dress, gravity has her sprawled face first against the teetering sliding glass door. Through the glass you see water rapidly approaching the balcony as the addition continues to tip. Her moav hard shell roller case is bouncing and smashes against the wall next to her, as the hotel room has gone from ninety to one hundred eighty degrees. The third and fourth floor crashes into the surge as the submerged bottom two floors are already breaking up. Wood is fragmenting while stucco and drywall are dissolving and disappearing into the water. It is a symphony of breaking glass, snapping wood, and lamenting humans. In short time the entire addition has split into a thousand pieces and has been dispersed around either side of the hotel, joining everything else on the eastern surge.

Following the impact of that second tsunami wave the water level is rapidly rising as the surge seems to be kicking up in amplitude. The waterline is halfway up the fourth story. All of the two story buildings surrounding the hotel are submerged. Arnold and Jim Morrison are nowhere to be seen. The stampede you heard previously was undeniably everyone on the fourth, fifth, and sixth floor running for the stairs and the roof. The unstoppable force created by dozens of humans has deflected hotel security from the roof deck stairwell entrance. A mob of Venetians and hotel guests spew forth from the industrial doorway. Standing space on the deck is immediately in short supply and dwindling.

Brian is standing near you as you clutch the surprisingly well anchored marble planter and deck sofa. Your eyes are locked with the French couple as you exchange a look of alarm and empathy. Baby Lyle is silent and seems to be in a wide eyed trance. Adriana is huddled behind the marble planter and Calvin is shielding her with his body. The manic force expelling through the stairwell door would make Black Friday shoppers look like geriatric antique scavengers. People are colliding and flung off edges into the black foam. Brian sees the inevitable approach of the masses, in his attempt to reach a more central section of the deck he balances himself by using his right arm to push off of your left shoulder.

As Brian is using your body to provide leverage for movement, the stitching on his left espadrille begins to unravel as he is screwing his foot into the deck. He purchased the footwear himself in Cusco, Peru on his way to Machu Picchu. He had "won" the vacation in a raffle put on by a vice president from one of the more prestigious media companies pitching to ByteBabble. Brian ensured the raffle was rigged for him to win, and in exchange the pitchman got some good business. Now lacking the necessary stitching, the cotton fabric of the upper portion of his casually cool footwear is no longer attached to the jute rope sole. With no support his foot slides off the sole, and slips on the wet surface of the deck. He is backpedaling with short, frenzied steps. Resembling someone breakdancing on a frozen sidewalk, his hands are grabbing for anything and touching nothing but cold moist pockets of air. It seems for a moment he might restore some semblance of balance, but adding insult to injury his right espadrille flips off his foot and spins end over end in space. Brian approaches the edge of the deck and falls on his backside with a significant teeth chattering thud, bounces a few inches off the floor, and falls off the western edge like a scuba diver rolling backwards off a boat.

Above, an LAPD Airbus H125 is jockeying for position below a hovering news chopper, the police spotlight strafing the roof of the hotel as the black and white helicopter circles the building in that familiar pattern. Brian is falling backwards towards the seething ebony liquid and a bed of unidentifiable chaff pushing against the hotel. He lands with a splashing crash. A jagged six foot piece of metal fencing pierces his back, spearing through his front near the right half of his collar bone. So many spinning rotors in close proximity are creating a thrumming similar to a car traveling at freeway speed with only one window open. The news helicopter bugs out after receiving a radio reprimand or spying the massive, raging fire towards the southern section of the Santa Monica Bay. The blaze is spectacular even from this distance and you're convinced it is the oil refinery in El Segundo.

Time slows again in your mind as you picture the oil platforms plaguing the coast of Carpinteria, Summerland, Santa Barbara and Goleta. God's country infested with offshore tumors, occasionally pumping coast killing cancer directly to the unsolicited marine life consumer. You recall disasters like the 1969 and 2015 Santa Barbara oil spills, forever altering the priceless geography and ecosystem. You indulge in a fantasy that just may be reality, picturing these horrific tsunami waves razing the offshore platforms, diminishing them to nothing but bad memories that will never be rebuilt as long as man's feet touch terra firma. Life snaps back to the reality at hand as the mass of people Brian attempted to avoid is reaching the western edge of the deck.

You brace against Adriana, who is holding on to Etienne, who is clutching his wife and child while Calvin stands pressing his back into the group with both arms outstretched horizontally. Resembling a flesh and blood plow, you are having some success deflecting the sad and unfortunate onslaught of humanity. Calvin is protecting the tip of the wedge with the ferocity of a third string running back trying to usurp the starter via a special teams performance.

Regrettably enough people have been displaced from the deck that it seems like there might be enough standing room for the remaining occupants. Just as everyone shows signs of slowing the brutal shuffle, a husky bearded two hundred pound red and black flannel clad man is ejected from the crowd. He arrives from the side and barrels into Etienne and Simone with significant force. Simone is clutching Lyle with the superhuman strength of a mother in distress, but the blanket that she is clutching rapidly unravels and sends Lyle spinning into the air. Lyle is rotating in an aerial pirouette five and a half feet off the roof and climbing. Below him the deck becomes a twenty foot drop to blackwater. Calvin explodes from his position, lunging with his left foot, thrusting forward and leaping off of his right foot. In an acrobatic mid-air feat Calvin is at full extension, palming Lyle's stripe capped head in his outstretched hand. He twists his body counterclockwise and shovel passes Lyle forcefully back in the direction he came from. Etienne and Simone shoot forth a combination of their four arms, catching Lyle and wrapping him in a desperate cocoon. Calvin continues his flight over the edge and cracks his head audibly against a very large beam floating in the water. Adorned with the helicopter spotlight, Calvin disappears into the depths.

Over an imperceptible amount of time Brian has floated east on Windward Ave amongst a bed of debris. The metal that has impaled him is lodged in the stripped interior of an abandoned car from Pacific Ave. He is helplessly attached to a Subaru whirling in a group of clanking, busted chassis. He notices the water is not as high as it was a few minutes ago when he observes the jackknifed frame of a Chevy Suburban jutting from the side of the building next to Hama Sushi. Quite a strange sight protruding from a third floor comprised mostly of large awning windows.

The surging water has eased its eastward push, and the inundation has become more of a choppy black lake. You look to the Santa Monica Bay and notice there is no discernable wave set. Instead it appears waves are moving in every direction, colliding with each other, and at some points offshore providing a whirlpool effect. You can see portions of the Venice pier when some of these rogue waves form their trough. Pilings are missing. The spotlights that were on the lifeguard headquarters no longer exist. The beach cities at Santa Monica Bay have been transformed into foamy, inky Lake Santa Monica. Now some of the debris is actually receding with the tide and flowing back out to sea.

Brian's rolling procession of destroyed automobiles catches the receding tide and begins to bob back towards Windward Ave. The tide has withdrawn enough that he can see the tattoo sign attached to the wall above the colonnade. The pain below his collarbone is relentless. He has swallowed a great deal of water, and he can taste the gasoline leaking all around him. He is in shock and surprised that he has not lost consciousness, his awareness certainly benefiting from large quantities of adrenaline. A palm that had been snapped near the base is receding faster than his group of cars. The palm strikes his Subaru like a giant Balabushka pool cue thumping into a billiard ball. The power of the collision forces the car onto its side, momentarily submerging Brian, as the auto bounces west down Windward Ave and lodges in the corner pocket that is the third floor patio of the Tattoo Addiction building (formerly Tattoo Asylum).

You make your way to the eastern edge of the hotel deck. You feel an enormous amount of guilt considering the ease at which you can now move about the rooftop. You pull your body above the stairwell door and climb an arrangement of large industrial fans to survey east of the hotel.

Six floors up you have an excellent vantage point. Panning from the northwest you scan down Rose Ave. Pockets of Santa Monica and most of Venice seem to be without power, but the streetlights on Pacific Ave still hum. The LAPD helicopter is performing a slow spotlight sweep southeast down Abbot Kinney Blvd. You think of the man himself, and wonder if Abbot Kinney would be pleased that his dream of Venetian canals in Los Angeles has now been extended to the 405 freeway. Off in the distance, past Lincoln Blvd, you see a hazy green glow that can only be Penmar Golf Course: the nine-hole course Harrison Ford used as an improvised runway for his restored World War II era Ryan Aeronautical ST3KR single engine airplane, when a loose part caused catastrophic engine trouble on March 5, 2015. The full moon is still jarringly bright despite the steady approach of morning. It is doing a decent job of illuminating your field of view, yet it is the alarming amount of dancing flame casting most of the glow on the geography.

Oh, the fire. Dozens of infernos spread across square miles of inundated Los Angeles. You can hear the cracking and howl of the flames kicking up thick plumes of black smoke. The sight conjures the unknown painter's *Great Fire of London* in 1666 and J.M.W. Turner's *The Burning of the Houses of Lords and Commons.* The juxtaposition of fire and water is both perplexing and amazing. Leonardo Da Vinci echoes in your mind:

"Fire destroys falsehood, that is sophistry, and restores truth, driving out darkness."

As you stand in bewilderment, a thirty foot 1994 Thor Industries Columbus RV appears amongst the debris heading back to the coast. Complete with a hydraulic leveling system, awning, booth dinette, and 454 Chevy motor, this once proud recreational vehicle had been undoubtedly serving as a dwelling for one of the hundreds or thousands of homeless lucky enough to live in their cars instead of inside a tent or across a mattress on the sidewalks of Venice. Lumbering with an uneven manner on a collision course with the Erwin or the Bank of Venice building next door, you know the impact will be nothing compared to the tsunami waves, and with your numbed senses you wear a blank mask and wait for the RV to get its final trip over with.

The RV is close enough that you can read the attempts at decal humor. "Wine drinker with a camping problem," "RV there yet," "If you lived in your car, you'd be home right now," "Mobile beach house," and "I'm Having an Out-of-Money Experience." While you're trying to stomach that last one the RV crashes at an angle into the northeastern corner of the Erwin, the southern wall of the Bank of Venice building, and a utility pole with a mounted transformer bank of three single phase transformers. The utility pole has had a long night, and either this was the straw that broke the camel's back, or the RV outright snapped the base. The transformers discharge sparks like they were crawling with miniature welders as the pole falls towards the Bank of Venice. The roof of what used to be the Santino's Pizza portion of the building provides a hard landing for the three transformers. They explode in a violent burst of blue and orange cannon fire. A pyrotechnician would be hard pressed to put together a more impressive display. A billow of sparks mushrooms above both buildings, hissing and dissipating in the sky while igniting pools of leaked gasoline and flammable chemicals pooled in the blackwater below. The fire quickly spreads to the countless beds of combustible materials that have collected against buildings and destroyed cars. You no longer question how fire could exist amongst so much water. Black smoke is already swirling from the upper windows on the east side of the Bank of Venice building.

In all of the madness you think there had been six power lines attached to the utility pole. Four of them are still attached to the pole, bouncing the pillar in the water as if it was a high voltage marionette. Two of the wires are downed and squirming about a flooded Pacific Ave, emitting loud pops with each flashing crack of the charged bullwhip. Suddenly, like some giant had lifted the rock it was hiding under, a blue-green red and orange trail of fire darts like a sidewinder around the building and west on Windward Ave.

Brian, skewered and attached to a Subaru wedged above a tattoo shop, is examining himself during his brief respite from the deluge. Steady blood loss and a mixture of sharp and deep throbbing pain make it almost impossible to comprehend what is happening, but the dire nature of his situation could not be clearer. The trail of fire that has just recently cornered onto Windward has ignited another bed of wood, mattress, and plastic. That fire acts as one candle lighting another and ignites debris collected inside the top floor of the building. This is compounding with the portion of the building that is already ablaze.

More black smoke billows from available openings as an ignited propane tank corkscrews from the wreckage in a stupefying trajectory a few feet above the floodwater. Spewing grey vapor and a propane jet flame, the rocket travels across Windward Ave and flies unhindered through one of the shattered windows of the Venice Beach Hostel. Almost immediately after this morbid hole-in-one orange light is flickering fiendish shadows off the walls, closely followed by black smoke.

The buildings of the northwest and southwest corners of Windward and Pacific are ablaze. Everything under the night sky has a bittersweet hue. The Nissan Rogue that was lodged across a column and storefront window is submerged below Brian's perch, just one of many vehicles that have been steadily leaking gasoline into the water.

Panic reaches a level that Brian did not know existed. From his forced position looking west he can only use light dancing off the buildings to gauge the proximity of the flames. Now he feels the elevated heat contributing additional discomfort to the throbbing agony of metal thrust through his body. With an abrupt sucking whoosh the scorching combustion of fossil fuels encircle Brian's zinc-coated steel sepulcher. His submerged legs don't have the space or energy to do more than twitch amok. The right side of his upper body is paralyzed with nerve damage and unmanageable pain. His spasming neck muscles jerk and thrust his skull about the wreckage. Brian's left arm is thrashing and churning flammable liquid while pumpkin and mahogany flames lick off blackwater, dancing on his whiplashing form. This is occurring out of your view and the source is unknown, yet you hear Brian's screams, the short time they last. The napalm sheen has liquefied Brian's skin and clothing as the metal around him begins to hum that strange warping sound and crack with the fire. Still whipping about, his lipless teeth emit a silent scream while they swiftly bite and chomp like a wind up chattering teeth toy. The demonic dance concludes as the charred corpse becomes motionless, reduced to lifeless carbon in the burning black liquid.

Windward Ave is a river of fire. The entire eastern façade of 21 Windward Ave is painted with a one hundred fifty by fifty foot mural by prolific Los Angeles artist Jonas Never. Titled *Touch of Venice*, the black and white masterpiece is an homage to Orson Welles' 1958 film noir classic *Touch of Evil*, where the once continuously colonnaded Windward Ave doubled as the Mexican border for Charlton Heston and Janet Leigh in one of the greatest opening shots in the history of film. Your vote for the finest example of street art in the city, and this morning at 21 Windward every window above the water line is vomiting fire. Once again gasps of despair and exhausted moans pull at your concentration like an unseen claw. You jump down from the industrial fans and scurry back towards the western portion of the deck. You are standing next to Adriana.

The water level is beginning to rise as the surface of the floodwater becomes increasingly irritated. Offshore in the darkness you see the shadow of a massive swell. This is not the forty foot tower of water that arrived as the second wave, but a more mysterious rolling bulge that continues to grow as the water level around you keeps rising. Your instincts are telling you this must be the tsunami coup de grâce. A sickening plunge in your stomach sends bile into the back of your mouth. Adriana turns her expressionless face towards you.

"I thought the world was supposed to end with a whimper."

There are no piers above the water line. There is no beach. All two story buildings in sight are disappearing again. The offshore swell has arrived and it is disgusting. As the swell proceeds it is collecting all of the trash, splintered wood, twisted metal, tree branches, bricks, broken concrete, shattered glass, rocks uprooted from the ocean floor, big screen televisions, leaked gasoline, refrigerators, fully intact rooves, vehicles of all body style, street signs, basketballs, loveseats, drywall, shopping carts, and corpses that had briefly moved west as water was sucked back to the ocean.

The swell encompasses the entirety of 21 Windward Ave with the vehement hiss of water on flame, white smoke bubbling into foam and escaping to the atmosphere. Seconds later the swell has reached the Erwin and is crashing a surge of debris into the façade ten feet below the roof.

"That wave's got to be fifty feet," exclaims an Estuary English accent in the crowd.

The swell moves on, and the giant rolling wave is extinguishing the burning buildings down Windward Ave. The blazing beds of debris are picked up and forced to surf this mammoth, glassy wave continuing east high above the submerged pavement.

You run back towards the industrial fans to pull and climb your way to the top. You do this partly for self-preservation and partly with a guilty vicarious pleasure that immediately disgusts you. Etienne, Simone, and Lyle have ducked into the industrial armor of the stairwell. This wave doesn't have the freight train boom shared by the other two, probably because you are watching it simply roll over and submerge everything. Practically your entire world is underwater. Only a handful of buildings are over the water line as you watch the back of the giant swell glide to the east. Pieces of debris are kicking off the top of the swell and rolling down its heaving back. From what you can gather, most of the debris is a flaring hostage swept east, its captor displaying no intention of relenting.

A deep buzzing oxblood has materialized on the horizon, melting away into burnt orange, supporting silhouetted clouds and a curved blue-black arch across the entire horizon

underneath everything that remains in the jet clutches of
Nyx. You've lost all semblance of time during this ordeal.
This dawn signals that ocean has been destroying your
territory for two hours.

From somewhere around Venice Blvd you hear a chorus of
deep, booming barking and question if there is some secret
and baleful close quarters Rottweiler breeder stealthily
operating in your neighborhood. Up to the north you see a
sliver of roof at the apartments famous for housing the actual
flesh and blood Jim Morrison, where Jim crashed courtesy of
his friend Danny Jacobs in the summer of 1965. The same
summer he sat on the beach with Ray Manzarek and shared
his poetry, birthing The Doors. The unremitting blackwater
deluge slips across that roof and for this moment effectively
ceases the existence of the landmark that is 14 Westminster
Ave. Almost directly across the street at 5 Westminster
Avenue is a six story building immortalized in the 1986 film
Cobra as the penthouse apartment of Sylvester Stallone's hard
boiled Marion Cobretti. You may remember the smooth
saxophone of Gloria Estefan & Miami Sound Machine as
Cobra returns home: sacrifices his newspaper in a charcoal
grill, uses scissors to cut himself a piece of pizza, and cleans
his gun with the kit he keeps refrigerated in an egg carton, all
while wearing his signature reflective sunglasses indoors.
You can clearly see the Cobra penthouse is unaffected. The
elements have discerning tastes and a sick sense of humor
when it comes to preservation.

Water continues to rush as the sun slowly rises. The breaking
swell has extended beyond your view, probably by now

thrusting flaming garbage and tormented souls against the notorious north-south Interstate 405. You ponder the irony of the most maligned freeway in Los Angeles being responsible for saving dozens, maybe hundreds, or even thousands of lives by eating the brunt of the wave and debris with its ramps, bridges, and walls. The ornery paved serpent cuts through the city at concrete heights of fifty feet at some points.

With the swell off in the distance your panorama is otherworldly. The terrain looks like God dropped a heavenly glass of blue-green black milk on the beach cities of Los Angeles. Those dogs are still barking. You revolve to the horizon, God's canvas under constant revision. Red has become orange as the clouds brush black and white across the skyline. That golden face, that sphere of fiery plasma, fills you with hope as it ascends. Shadows of seagulls blink across.

Powerboats, sailboats, and yachts are voyaging inland. Thankfully none of them have plotted course for the Erwin, but the sight of pleasure craft east of Pacific Ave is discomforting nonetheless. There are not many buildings above the waterline to impede navigation. These boats were obviously formerly anchored in Marina Del Rey. The tsunami waves and rising tide made short work of the inlet rock barriers and breakwaters, easily transporting vessels over seawalls. The stern of a wooden forty-eight foot 1974 Rumery 48 identifies itself as the *Dock Holiday* as it floats backwards towards the east. Onboard one man stands on the bridge holding on for dear life, boasting an expansive sclera dominated thousand-yard stare. You recognize him as one of the bartenders at The Galley on Main St in Santa Monica.

Suddenly sixty feet of steel rears from the drink like a roused Leviathan. *Declaration* must have been clunking end over end on the underwater avenues. The force of this final surge pushes the sculpture upwards with one arm crashing down onto the southwest deck of the Erwin. Tracing the deck in a semi-circle like an arbitrating compass, the metal arm wipes five people into the water, including a husky, flannel clad bearded man.

Minutes after this freakish display the waters become virtually calm for a half a moment. Just as you think your heart has reached its limitations a distant sound begins to rumble. The inundation is returning to the sea. Looking east you see the burning perimeter of inferno spread far and wide by that final swell.

Returning to you is a reverse tsunami of everything you saw driven inland and more. After a short period of time mountains of burning material, entire bungalows, cars, trucks, RVs, deracinated trees, females, males, rich, poor, sheltered, homeless, black, white, brown, beige and everything in between are moving towards you at frightening speed. The crashing of debris, creaking of materials, and rushing of water is making up for what the swell lacked in decibel level on its trip east. This is all occurring up close and personal due to the obscene height of the waterline brought on by the final surge.

Your brain and soul relent as you unmount the block of fans and press your body and head against their side, closing your eyes and covering your ears. The crashing is still audible, and every impact is felt. This seems to last for a solid ten minutes, but in your state you have no idea if the actuality was what you perceived.

8

Calvin is underwater floating southwest on California Ave.
He passes a house that used to have a curbside hoop he'd use
with his childhood friends. He slips across Abbot Kinney
Blvd and travels southeast on Andalusia Ave, west on Grand
Blvd and then south on Riviera Ave towards that excuse for
modern architecture he used as a stash house, paying a
monthly amount to the homeowner behind on his mortgage.
He journeys west on Venice Blvd by the apartment building
where he had to kidnap a transplant from Chicago who made
the mistake of selling in Venice. Now above a subaqueous
network of canals, where he had the little homie bust that
yuppie in the nose for that iPhone. He is slipping down Dell
Ave, then west on Washington Blvd past Cabo Cantina,
passing the sad image of an underwater Hinano Cafe, and
reaching the Whaler, formerly a most lucrative place of
business. He nears the Venice pier and the water is no longer
so dark. Morning's rising sun sends shimmering beams of
dazzling white that pierce the water's surface. Flickering
fingers of light surrounding Calvin, carrying him out,
carrying him back, accepting him to the depths.

After another unknown amount of time filled with silent
embraces, sobbing, and comatose body language you hear the
chopping blade of the LAPD helicopter. The aircraft is near
the Santa Monica and Venice border where Neilson Way
becomes Pacific Ave. The loudspeaker proclaims as it
approaches.

"Shelter in place. Assistance is on the way. Shelter in place. Assistance is on the way."

The helicopter passes the Erwin and flies south over the peninsula located west of the Marina and south of Washington Blvd. You have no doubt the entire peninsula is destroyed. You'd be surprised if even the sand remained, let alone the townhouses and condos. There is a chance for some of the massive apartment and condominium complexes in the Marina, like the Shores on Via Marina, and maybe the Marquesas, Panay, and Palawan Way buildings. The chance is slim considering you see no sign of their existence, although you maintain hope considering they are two miles from your location, and it is difficult to draw a bead on any structures through the curtain of smoke and scattered flame.

The remaining drone hovers above Windward Circle for thirty seconds and then zips to the southeast. All of the water planning on returning to the sea has already made its homecoming. The remainder lurks in giant pools of murk surrounded by stubborn crackling fire and a ludicrous amount of refuse. You think of the homeless encampment that previously surrounded all four sides of the Public Storage building on Rose and 3rd Ave. Every single walkway, street, and neighborhood in your field of view makes the former Public Storage encampments look like finely manicured Singapore sidewalks in comparison.

You wouldn't need more than one hand to count the structures that might still be habitable. You can see the apartment building you forewent on Speedway and Venice.

On Washington Blvd the eight story monolith that is the Studio (MDR) ™ stands strong and tall in a wavering haze of heat and smoke. That ten story retail residential building on Washington and Dell Ave is still there. The Marina Del Rey Marriot remains defiantly, but you know there won't be any more tourist dollars to sustain it. Cobra can still scissor the corner off one piece of pizza for dinner, the alabaster walls of his Waldorf penthouse are reflecting the new day's sun.

Virtually every other building in your field of view has some form of catastrophic damage. If one of the walls isn't caved in, the roof has been torn off, or floodwater has simply ripped the structure from its foundation and relocated the domicile free of charge. If a residence is not currently converted into a raging pyramid of fire it has been damaged beyond repair by water, chemicals, debris impact, or a palm tree ramming through a living room window and out the kitchen door to the backyard. You actually recognize the one hundred and ten foot yacht, the *Liquid Asset*, which once sailed you and your cohort around the marina on a booze cruise. Now this failed ark has decided to precariously anchor atop the remaining half of a roof sheltering what used to be the Venice post office. The entire city of Venice is destroyed.

The air is thick with the stench of sewage, fish, seawater, toxic gases, smoke, and death. Observing the smoldering holocaust from your roost atop the Erwin you feel like you're standing next to the main figure in John Martin's *Pandemonium*. Instead of an assembly of demons before you, a throng of corpses has congregated. Determining the age, sex, or standing of each person is too difficult and you can't bring yourself to look at this waste of humanity for more than a few seconds. You can't process the spectacle. Your mind starts to distract itself by instead focusing on the mangled car wrecks dotting the landscape, but you know it is a ploy executed internally. Your knees give out and you barely manage to catch your hand on the roof surface before you gag and vomit. Self-preservation kicks in again and you know this is especially bad considering how dehydrated you must be.

Faintly howling sirens are ever so slowly increasing in volume. They are deep in the distance. These first responders will probably take hours to get from Culver City to the coast. You reach into the sandwich bag. It is 7:30 a.m. You know your apartment is destroyed, but you want to see what state it's in. You also need water before you pass out or have some kind of panic attack seizure. You look out at the ocean and the water is almost behaving like a normal day at the beach, only there is a strange whirlpool a few hundred feet offshore with a small boat slowly circling the perimeter. The Venice lifeguard headquarters is standing as it always has, except the windows have been blown out and the metal garage doors have been ripped off. Whatever lifeguard vehicles formerly housed in the garage are somewhere around Lincoln Blvd by now. The front third of the Venice pier has snapped and lies hunched in the ocean, pilings are noticeably missing. The Santa Monica pier looks like it is being supported by an unsafe number of pilings as well, and the entire surface is covered in wreckage. The Venice Skate Park has been filled with sand. The beach has been completely transformed and filthy black sand extends beyond Pacific Ave.

The decision has been made, your exhausted body heads for the stairwell. Lyle's penetrating blue eyes. You look back at the huddled mass of a family that has survived the worst disaster they will ever see, through miraculous fortune and the selfless sacrifice of one man. Most of those remaining on the roof are still frozen in fear, and a few, including Adriana, follow you down the stairwell.

The lobby of the Erwin is knee deep with debris. That tricolored couch is nowhere to be found, and only one surfboard remains, spread horizontally across the lobby restaurant's espresso machine and liquor shelf. You wade through the debris and turn right heading south down Pacific Ave. You can't even look to your left and right to acknowledge what you've been staring at these past few hours on the roof. Complete survival mode.

Two hundred feet south of the Erwin at Pacific and Mildred Ave the skeleton of a Ford Excursion is heaving black pollution as it smolders in a puddle of burning liquid, covering half the street. You hear the heavy slapping of twenty-eight limbs splashing forcefully in whatever wet mess coats the street. Whooping and barking the same roar you heard earlier, seven northbound beasts slalom the destroyed vehicle. They are each collared with a crude knotted rope, and each leash of the rope leads back into one giant knot dragging behind them. One monster stops to sniff a corpse and is immediately wrenched back into formation by the tensed rope around its neck. These roaring animals, it is impossible to determine what pedigree of oversized attack hounds have been utilized here. An instinctual reflex causes you to dash laterally towards the ruins of a brick wall on the east side of Pacific Ave. Thankfully the pack charges up Pacific without saluting you. You move around the Excursion while looking behind you, and to your horror they come upon Adriana. The hairs on the back of your neck stand up as the beasts surround her. You are astonished at her lack of fear as she snaps up the connecting knot and pulls tight. She is standing there drawing on the improvised braided rope reins as the beasts encompass her and pose in place, maintaining their aggressive posture with jowls pulled back and massive fangs dripping and gleaming, heaving their torsos as they fervently exhale steaming breath. Her red and black hair picks up a breeze as you lock with her vibrant eyes before smoke and flame kick up from the Excursion to hinder your sightline.

Withdrawing towards your apartment you persistently lament the state of affairs. The sunshine casts an unflinching light on what has become of your neighborhood. The three tenths of a mile previously covered in quick strides is now fifteen hundred feet of unpredictable hazard. You slowly and deliberately make your way, conceding you are not at full capacity. Soon you are on the east side of Pacific Ave, across from the Canal Club, staring directly west at a mural of Charlie Chaplin. Painted with varying shades of blue, Chaplin is facing you with his deadpan expression, his chin resting on the curved top of his cane. To the left of Charlie is a white block letter one word sentence. SMILE. You are amongst four people in close proximity to this image, and the only one standing upright. You are lost in this visage for some time. Your mind drifts to the Canal Club fight scene carried out by Sean Penn and Glenn Plummer in the 1988 film *Colors;* directed by Dennis Hopper, another son of Venice. You know this is another mental ploy to distract you. Your brain is aware there is no coping with this situation.

Reaching the intersection of South Venice Blvd and Pacific Ave you stumble upon an organism you never wanted to encounter in the wild. The stuff of nightmares, now impotent out of its element, a seven foot juvenile great white shark, mouth ajar, lies prone on the cracked asphalt concrete of Venice Blvd. Unbelievable. You succumb to the urge and brandish your phone to take a photo for posterity. Focus, HDR, framing, snap. As you hold the phone before you a spark, ember, or pop of electricity hits a broken gas line in the kitchen of the Canal Club. The explosion grinds sand into your eyeballs before you can close the lids. An unknown form of debris peppers the right side of your face with a biting sting. You are thrown from your feet and onto the left side of your body, bonking your head off the puddled pavement beside the shark.

Rolling onto your back you groan through clenched teeth. You can't see. It takes minutes for you to blink and rub sight back into the equation. You are aware of the bacteria you just kneaded into your eyes, but at least you landed on the side of your body that wasn't bleeding from the street shrapnel. No one is around to see this, no one is around to help, and no one is around to care. No one but the landlord of the ocean stinking beside you. The man in the grey suit. His lifeless black eye judging your stupidity.

You are alive. You suck it up, angry at your rookie behavior. Spending five minutes looking for your phone you decide it is a fruitless endeavor. It's a needle in a haystack amongst all this debris, and by now there is enough water damage that it's a sapphire crystal drink coaster. You shuffle the remaining tenth of a mile and stand before your apartment building.

9

The front door to your building has been ripped off the hinges. The hallway extends to the rear wall and a pile of debris stacked floor to ceiling. The briny aroma of floodwater has overpowered the usual bouquet of skunk reefer. The floor is a swamp. You climb the stairs and unlock your deadbolt. As you open the door a gush of murky liquid streams from you apartment and cascades down the stairs. The seal on the door has surprised you with its fortitude. The water is nearly waist height as you step back and let the apartment drain.

What a mess. All of your furniture has been inverted and rearranged in a sick display of tsunami feng shui. The windows are smashed and the Venetian blinds are scattered throughout. Living room furniture is stacked in the bedroom and bedroom furniture is pressed against the west wall of your kitchen. Not a fan of the décor, but your perpetual gratitude for life yields little self-pity. The stream of floodwater begins to slow and you take inventory. The TV is shattered and face down in the corner of the living room. All of your books have been turned to pulp. Filing cabinets have been emptied, glass and porcelain litter the floor. The refrigerator is in the living room. You spy with your little eye a beech wood handled butterfly knife with a three and a half inch blade. Saint-Tropez and the image of a small sailing yacht is carved into the handle. You bought this in 2015 at a souvenir shop in Ramatuelle on your second tour of the Côte d'Azur. With mild amusement you remember coyishly daring French, Swiss, and American customs as you placed it in your one checked bag and departed Nice for a Zurich layover before the non-stop to Los Angeles. You remember the Swiss customs agents looking at you, eyeing your American passport, whispering to each other, and moving you along. Undetected, or not worth the trouble. There was no incident in Los Angeles either, perhaps because you were playing it cool on a heavy cocktail of beer, Remy Martin XO, and five milligrams of alprazolam. The only way to fly.

The balisong gets wiped off and slips into your jean pocket. You crack open the fridge and collect five bottles of water. Immediately guzzling two, the third is used to pour across the cuts left by the debris and shrapnel. There is a plastic bottle of dish soap in a wet patch on the floor and you use that to soap up your face and upper body, doing your best to ignore the discomfort. Half of the fourth bottle goes into your stomach and the other half rinses off the soapy film covering your face. You feel worse for wear, but in the grand scheme of things you're on four hours of sleep and it's not like you stormed the beach at Normandy. You feel fortunate that this has been more mentally damaging than physically, and every two minutes in the apartment you stop to thank God.

In the kitchen you rifle through the cupboard and find some crunchy peanut butter and chocolate chip Clif Bars, making short work of three on the spot and washing them down with the fifth and final bottle of water. There is not much to be salvaged upon surveying the bedroom. The entire closet was underwater at some point, but the hanging clothes and top shelves were at least not under constant assault. You stuff as many socks, underwear, pants, shirts, and jackets as you can fit into your duffel bag. A feeling of elation accompanies the sight of your Bianchi road bike hanging undamaged on the ceiling hook. You snatch your Fox Head Flux Savant bike helmet and strap it to your dome. Duffel bag over your shoulder you lean down and overturn your combination locked cabinet. Most of the files have been converted to mash, but your U.S. Passport has displayed resilience and slides into your pocket. You snap open the blue plastic case at the bottom of the drawer and pull out the Smith and Wesson 686 Plus .357 Magnum revolver. Four inch barrel, three pounds of stainless steel with a black rubber grip, this L-framed revolver has been built to withstand more than water. You purchased this firearm when you were employed and the home invasions really started to pick up steam. The duffel bag gets topped off with fifty Remington Golden Saber 125-Grain brass jacketed .357 magnum hollow point cartridges and one hundred Remington UMC 130-Grain .38 Special full metal jacket cartridges.

Duffel bag heavy on your back, helmet strapped in, you grab the hydroformed aluminum frame and lift the Italian bicycle equivalent of an F-35 Lightning from the hook in your bedroom. You lean the bike against the hallway as you lock your deadbolt, not knowing when you will return to your home, or to this beautiful city turned disaster area. Carrying the bike down the stairs you place both wheels on the pavement and once more head north on Pacific Ave, this time turning right and walking your bike east on South Venice Blvd.

10

Countless times you have rendered yourself high as an elephant's eye and cycled from Venice to Hollywood and back. Usually reaching Sunset Blvd and Fairfax Ave before returning west to complete the thirty or forty mile "puff and pedal." The passing scenery was like your own personal music video, as your headphones would blast whatever was floating your boat at the time. Anyone can point out the obvious negative aspects of Los Angeles, but no one can deny that this is a city of beautiful people. Your vote for number one, and on these rides it's like you're falling in love every one hundred feet. There are few things you'd rather do on a summer Saturday.

Most of your friends within striking distance live in one bedroom apartments or have roommates. Your plan is to ride just east of Central Los Angeles to Koreatown and the two bedroom apartment rented by Terry Barnes. Terry was your coworker close to a decade ago and you bonded over so many hilarious and outrageous adventures, the type that only cities like Los Angeles or New York can provide. He is a stand up dude from Buffalo, NY and it is obvious he was raised in a tight knit family that drove home those fundamental values. Six months ago the guy renting Terry's second bedroom couldn't work after a motorcycle crash and had to head back to Arkansas or Missouri. You are almost certain he will let you briefly reside in the spare room, and it's either this bike ride or taking a chance in whatever tent city forms out of this wasteland. The duffel bag is heavy and will make it difficult to remain balanced, but considering this is just a one way trip compared to your epic rides you're confident there will be no problems. Venice Blvd is actually a straight shot to Koreatown, but you're going to plot a course north and then east to avoid this perilous badland.

You continue to walk your bike east on Venice Blvd due to the amount of obstacles, debris, and water spread across the wide thoroughfare. You anticipate the buildings that line the smaller north south streets will have blocked some debris. After two miles and close to an hour you are at Venice and Walgrove Ave. Walgrove is the first main street that extends north, and you know it reaches higher elevation as you approach the Santa Monica Airport off of Ocean Park Blvd.

There are no operating cars, no moving people, and no first responders. You're pushing on, yet you are fully conscious that you are in an emotional state of shock. The abandoned, destroyed city littered with palm fronds and corpses feels like a scene from George Romero's *Day of the Dead*. Your heart is racing when you hallucinate a twitching leg connected to one of the corpses. Time to get on the bike.

Slow deliberate movement, but faster than a jog. You're changing to an easier gear as you climb elevation where Walgrove becomes 23rd St. Up you go over a succession of three hills, reaching the top of the mesa that is this portion of Santa Monica geography. You see your first operating auto, a BMW X5 travelling west down Pico Blvd. You cut through Virginia Park and up Cloverfield Blvd. A few hundred feet and you are crossing the eastbound Interstate 10 freeway. North of the 10 the damage is minimal and you feel like you've just entered another dimension. You cut east on the Arizona Ave bike lane between Wilshire and Santa Monica Blvd.

This is ludicrous. The environment is practically business as usual. You pass four parked Santa Monica Police SUVs with their lights spinning red and blue. The officers are standing outside of the vehicles with their hands on squawking radios. Are they waiting for a gameplan? At this point your focused mission replaces any other thought processes with complete indifference.

On autopilot, you've become accustomed to the heavy duffel. You cross the 405 at Santa Monica and Sepulveda Blvd. The intersection is humming with traffic as you get the feeling these people are commuting to work. The anger fuels you and you're in that zone people refer to as the "runner's high." Continuing on the wide bike lane, you arrive in Beverly Hills. You pass Beverly Gardens Park and the massive oak tree at Rodeo Dr and Santa Monica Blvd. Resting at its trunk one afternoon you listened to the tree drop acorns into the dirt in a musical sequence that legitimately seemed like it was communicating with you. The serenity of the oak calms you slightly.

South of the Sunset Strip you turn right and head east on Melrose Ave. Five more miles. The final gauntlet.

Melrose and Western Ave. You bank right like a jetfighter and the duffel almost throws you off balance. Stupid. All downhill now. There goes Beverly Blvd. Western and 3rd St.

You're in Koreatown. Western and 6th St. The strip mall signs advertise eleven businesses each, and every word is in Korean except Liquor and Dentist. Another world.

Zipping by the Koreatown Plaza you recall how it opened for business one year before the 1992 Los Angeles riots. You remember the proud, brave Korean Los Angelenos brandishing firearms and standing guard at that very building, as the LAPD abandoned them to protect more affluent, influential portions of Los Angeles. Oh, the parallels.

Two intersections south of the Plaza you bank left on Olympic Blvd, and then down S Oxford Ave to arrive at your destination.

The apartment building is classic Los Angeles. The two story building has four two-bedroom apartments. The architecture is basically two cubes with the center of the structure consisting of a second floor walkway and a stone staircase. The walls are blue stucco and there are bars on the windows. There is a white and blue triangle tile design running from roof to foundation on the inner edges of each apartment cube. It is a clean, well maintained building with air conditioning. Terry is paying nine hundred dollars each month. For a two bedroom apartment in Los Angeles this is the steal of the century.

Stepping off your ivory steed you guide it gently to its side on top of the two foot plot of grass between the sidewalk and the street. Terry is on the second floor with his elbows resting on the thin metal railing. He is smoking an American Spirit cigarette with the blue pack balanced on the railing beside him. He takes his lean off the railing and displays an expression of surprise and then relief.

"Dude, I've been calling you."

"Where are the Newports, city boi?"

11

Laughing as he descends the stairs Terry resembles Joe Louis
or a young Muhammad Ali if they had some Creole blood.
He is wearing a Miami Pawn Shop t-shirt, designer jeans, and
a pair of black boots that cost as much as the average monthly
car payment.

You dip your shoulder and slide off the duffel bag, clap right
palms with Terry and embrace.

"Can I crash here for a minute?"

"No doubt. Mi casa, su casa. Hit the shower."

Terry picks up your duffel bag as you shoulder your bike and
climb the stairs. His two bedroom apartment is spacious
with white walls and white carpet. Bright and welcoming,
there are some thriving green plants beside a white leather
couch and glass coffee table that faces a television. Terry's
kitchen is to the left of his dining area, which has a nice south
and west facing pair of windows as it occupies that corner of
the building. You are heading down the hallway and turning
the corner into the bathroom as Terry tosses you a Hurricane
Football t-shirt and a pair of black Jumpman basketball
shorts. Judging by the length of the leg, the shorts look like
they pre-date the era of the late two thousand teens when
foolish men decided it was a good idea to slowly regress
towards the John Stockton hot pants style. The dark
pendulum of fashion. A smile curls as you remember Terry
telling you once:

"As far as I'm concerned, you're an honorary Hurricane... the only one I know out here playing life helmet to helmet!"

Terry was a high school quarterback in Buffalo before the U converted him to wide receiver, and then a practice squad special teams tackling apparatus. This was during the super stacked squads boasting the likes of Andre Johnson and Reggie Wayne. He prided himself on once charming a young lady before a future NFL running back could complete his own sales pitch. In 2020 his bones are still creaking from his attempted tackle being ferociously broken by a punt returning Ed Reed. He embraces the CITY BOI nickname bestowed by some of his rural teammates who had honed their craft and stoked their speed chasing hares through the burning cane fields of south Florida.

You are painting the enamel of Terry's bathtub black with all varieties of dirt, grime, muck, salt, sweat, and congealed blood. Washing your hair is almost indescribably refreshing but you still feel like hammered compost. The entire shower is spent thanking God that you're alive, questioning the reasons you survived, and replaying the images of Calvin and Lyle, the hounds turning the corner on the Excursion, the pandemonium of destruction, the faces frozen with terror, the lifeless bodies. That shark.

Now showered and sitting on the couch, Terry reaches into the hall cupboards and tosses you three blankets. He pulls up a chair and crosses his legs, rolling a joint with a small pile of ground cannabis and tobacco that rests on a cinematography book. You're using his cell phone to text those who matter, and asking them to notify everyone whose number you can't remember.

"I am safe at a friend's apartment. Resting now. Hit me on email."

You lie down as Terry is sparking the flint and holding the joint in his mouth, raising his chin in an offering nod and asking via his expression. You decline and feel the firm grip of Morpheus taking control. Terry flips on the news while you doze off.

"This is unreal. I know you are that rare breed, but damn, you are lucky. Someone has a plan for you."

Jessica Winchester is back in that same red blazer with tasteful cleavage.

"This morning at 3:15 a.m. Pacific Standard Time a 9.2 magnitude earthquake occurred two hundred miles off the coast of Southern California. U.S. Geological Survey seismologists are adamant that a so called megathrust earthquake is the only type of known terrestrial source of tectonic activity that can produce magnitude of this scale. Seismologist Sally Barnwhistle is currently briefing the media:

'Megathrust earthquakes occur when one tectonic plate is forced underneath another. Pressure builds until the bending top plate "flicks" off the bottom one, thrusting upward and creating massive force. Every single recorded earthquake over a magnitude of 9.0 has been a megathrust earthquake.

Theoretically a megathrust earthquake could occur in the ocean off the coast of Oregon and Washington, where the Pacific Plate meets the Juan De Fuca Plate in an area we call the Cascadia Subduction Zone. A megathrust earthquake at that location could exceed a magnitude of 9.0. The thrusting plate could create tsunami waves of over one hundred feet.

What I personally find so troubling is that for a megathrust earthquake to occur in Southern California you would need the Pacific Plate to overlap the North American Plate. The thing is, these plates meet at the San Andreas Fault, which as you all know is inland thirty-five miles east of Los Angeles, not two hundred miles off the coast. So we're going to need to look into this pretty thoroughly, and maybe reassess everything we know about plate tectonics. I might also add that we are in dire need of funding as our federal budget has been drastically cut by large percentages three consecutive years.

Now, what we do know is that a 9.2 magnitude earthquake occurred two hundred miles west of Los Angeles. This created a seismic sea wave also known as a tsunami. We believe that this series of waves experienced an increase in amplitude due to a massive underwater landslide caused by the earthquake. We think this is why you saw tsunami waves of over sixty feet in some portions of Southern California.

That is all of the information I can provide at this moment. We are actively investigating this phenomenon. Thank you.'

That was Sally Barnwhistle with the U.S.G.S. providing some very disturbing facts. First responders are currently working the area. If you are in Los Angeles, and are available to give blood, please use the number or website at the bottom of your screen.

This is a developing emergency situation, please stay tuned for updates. We have no estimates in regards to loss of life or property damage involving the three hundred thousand people living in the tsunami inundation zone.

We are going to go to our very own Charles Skeeler who is at the Los Angeles Fire Department Station 43 in Culver City. Chuck?"

Terry turns off the TV once he sees that you are asleep. He heads out to the stairway with a gingerade kombucha and an American Spirit.

You dream that you're back in Venice, lying in bed watching headlights flash across your bedroom wall. The wall at your feet falls forward like it was made of foam board. A waterfall of blackwater explodes into your bedroom, bouncing off the remaining walls and filling the room until you wake up sucking air in a cold sweat.

You pour a glass of filtered water and lean against the wall in the grey city light, staring out the south window.

The periodic whooshing of nighttime traffic on Olympic Blvd reminds you of the ocean. You thank God again.

12

Today marks ten days since the disaster took 26,181 lives and displaced close to one million individuals across Southern California. A preposterously underfunded FEMA is moving at the snail's pace ensured by bureaucracy. Your home and every building in the area has been condemned. The Marina Del Rey Marriot and Ritz Carlton hotels have been converted to temporary housing for families that have been displaced, no doubt in return for a massive tax write off for the multinational corporation that owns both hotels. The first four floors of both hotels are uninhabitable, not much of a dent in the number of displaced. FEMA has shipped some of the unemployed victims to temporary housing in Oregon, Nevada, and Arizona. It seems the majority of victims are cursed to scrape by in the tent cities that have popped up all over Los Angeles County. It has only been a week and a half but there are already reports of fighting, theft, rape, human trafficking, and more than one murder. FEMA is providing bottled water and "meals ready to eat," but little else. There are barely any police in the whole county, and an almost non-existent presence protecting the inhabitants of these encampments. Social media has provided enough glaring evidence of this that the main stream media cannot ignore the facts. The beach cities might have been the only area directly touched by the wave system, but the entirety of the city is feeling the unrelenting grip around its throat. It is a cold hard fact that your city, your state, and your federal government lack the means to solve the crisis.

You still have all your fingers and toes, and you still draw breath while the sun rises in the sky, so you decide to step out into the warm fall day and get some exercise. Maybe some vitamin D will improve your mood. You are clearly suffering from PTSD, plagued by nightmares experienced every night on the futon in Terry's spare bedroom.

Los Angeles has its reputation as that glorious summertime beach destination, but as an Angeleno you know fall is the finest time of year. When most of the country is starting to get hints of winter chill, your city is enjoying dark blue skies and eighty degrees Fahrenheit. The summer rush of tourists have all gone back to school and work, leaving the land to the locals. Today is one such day, and you decide to cycle Sunset Blvd through West Hollywood, Beverly Hills, and take San Vicente Blvd all the way west.

Gliding by all of the landmarks, all of your old haunts, you can't help but notice somewhat of a defeatist attitude in the body language of the people you pass. The everyday citizens going about their day seem as despondent as the homeless and afflicted. You arrive at Palisades Park and take a draw off the drinking fountain, balancing your bike against a bench at the rose garden north of Montana and Ocean Ave. Your first time back at the coast since the calamity.

The simple beauty of a rose reminds you nature never gets depressed. Before you are thirteen garden plots with a variety of red, orange, pink, lavender, yellow, and white roses. From your vantage point on the bench the sun is choreographing rose petals in a translucent ballet of light as the waves crash on the mutated beach one hundred feet below. You walk to the stone railing overlooking the highway and ocean. Pacific Coast Highway has been cleared for traffic, bulldozers and trucks still comb the transformed coastline, attempting to reform its shape. South on PCH you see a hubbub of restoration at the Jonathan Club, a private social club catering to the upper crust since 1895. You walk back towards a bust dedicating the rose garden to Arcadia Bandini de Baker, the woman who donated this precious land to the public in the early twentieth century. You sit at a bench acknowledging you're probably seated in one of the most beautiful points on the globe, and you have your health, yet you can't shake the absence of hope.

With your head in your hands you think back to your life ten years in the past. It was only a few years after the peak of the Global Financial Crisis, but even during the crisis you were achieving promotions at your company. You had saved enough money to travel to Europe for the first time. You fondly remember your twenty-four hour layover in Madrid, a masterful stroke of the keyboard as you booked flights covering a swathe of the continent. You suppose nothing got solved in the smoke and mirror economic recovery in the years to follow, and now your mind is predominantly on the wave that took almost everything you have.

"Thinking the big thoughts, huh?"

You are startled by an old man sitting beside you in a lightweight khaki jacket. He has the wise face of an old Italian and a full head of white hair parted on the left. He is wearing vintage tear drop style eyeglasses, and you are put to ease when you realize those are the brown robes of a Franciscan underneath his jacket.

"Yes... there's a lot to think about these days," you reply.

The man doesn't say anything, he just turns his head towards you and stares at your face for half a minute. He turns forward again and then juts out his arms in a broad extension. Stretching and expelling a noise that sounds like a roaring baby dinosaur, the man's right arm is extended behind your back and his left arm is pointing towards the ocean. Completing his stretch he speaks again.

"Yeah. My name is Father Virgil. I'm visiting St. Monica's over there on California Ave. Beautiful. I'm usually up at the Mission in Santa Barbara."

He folds his hands and tilts his head back, smiling face towards the sun.

"You never know how often an old man is going to clap eyes on the sea. Every time is a blessing. What's eating you?"

"The world," you reply. "The right path. Purpose."

Basking in the sun with his face towards the sky, the old man's eyes are squinting shut as he softly laughs to himself. Through a smile he starts to speak again.

"For God so loved. For God so loved this world."

His words are spoken with a passionate vigor despite his sunbathing configuration.

"Whoever believes should not perish, but have everlasting life."

Now he is looking you dead in the eye.

"You have to understand. I can tell by looking at you, you need to understand that there is always light in this world. We may experience life when it seems impossible to be the person who is good, but you and I both know you are not the darkness."

Shifting on the bench he is gesturing emphatically with his hands.

"Listen to me, I'm almost finished. Those who embrace darkness fear light because it will prove the evil of their deeds. Look at me. All you are is a sum of your actions. When your true action comes to light, this will be your salvation. You must believe this."

You are sitting on the bench in that uncanny October sunshine, dazed like you caught a stiff jab unseen on approach. Now Fr. Virgil is preparing to stand, his palms are on his knees.

"That part of you that was born flesh, is flesh; and that part of you that was born spirit, well, I think you understand."

The old friar is standing and facing you.

"I know that's pretty heavy for a Sunday bike ride... and I know you heard me."

One last stretch for the old man that loves the sea.

"Now if you'll excuse me, I work Sundays."

Off he walks. Your reaction is visceral as you sit there for some time before you make the return ride to Koreatown.

13

The ride home is perfectly timed as you enjoy golden hues bathing the tempered glass of Westwood skyscrapers and the gleaming orange reflections of the magic hour that is sundown. Reinvigorated and inspired after the rose garden you climb the stone stairwell in Koreatown and place your bike in Terry's kitchen. You are feeling slightly guilty, almost as if you're taking advantage of a friend, but Terry has been so gracious with his hospitality and you both know there are few options. You walk down the hallway to see Terry clacking away on his keyboard in front of what he calls the Matrix, an arrangement of six LED computer monitors on permanent loan from your previous employer.

"What's crackin', city boi?"

Terry laughs, "Hey. Working on Sunday. I'm just finishing up. Todd is going to come through in a little bit."

Terry works for a renewable energy company founded by business magnate, engineer, inventor, and investor Peter Triton. Three monitors consist of spreadsheets and presentation software while the other three exhibit a variety of playful women drifting face down on pool floats shaped like champagne bottles, donuts, and swans, beads of water sparkling off their tan unclothed skin.

"How do you get anything done?"

"Same way you get to Carnegie Hall. Go rustle up some steaks or something, we're going to watch *America Primetime.*"

A cool gust escaping the fridge feels nice on your skin as you look inside. Terry has bought three bone-in ribeyes from the Ralphs supermarket on Western, by the Wiltern Theater. Ralphs supermarkets have the best price to quality ratio for your taste, and you notice Terry benefited from close to a fifty percent price discount as the meat was approaching the sell-by date. Nonetheless, the price tag still shocks you; you will never become accustomed to the brutal stagflation gripping your country in this economic depression. You are thankful Terry is spreading the wealth and splurging on some Sunday steaks for his friends, and honestly you're thankful to have a roof overhead and be eating at all.

Three pads of butter and three glorious cuts of vitamin rich sliced carcass hit the skillet with a sizzle that's almost as good as the steak. The screen door rattles open and Todd Fenton has arrived in Koreatown. He is lugging a backpack and wearing a gold knit Lakers beanie, black wife-beater, black sweats, purple and gold Lakers socks, and a black pair of Adidas Ultra Boost running shoes.

"What do you call that style of shirt?"

"Tank top."

"Not a wife-beater?"

"That's pretty antiquated, my friend."

You clap right palms with Todd. Todd is all sinew with leading man good looks. People who make his acquaintance usually dismiss him as the quintessential blonde jock until they realize he is the smartest guy in the room. He attended Brown University on a football scholarship and studied history. A very interesting and unorthodox individual, Todd found moderate success as a member of a punk and bluegrass band, and significant success supplying the medical marijuana dispensaries of Los Angeles with hashish. This was before California voted to pass Proposition 64 in November of 2016, effectively legalizing recreational cannabis. These days Todd is the founder of Fight + Flight Fitness, and all around good guy, making a conscious effort to be a source of positivity and health.

"Where's the binger?"

"You know Terry doesn't have a bong."

"That I do."

Todd places his backpack on the dining area table and brandishes a two foot glass tube with low down ice pinches and a diffused downstem. You hear Terry lumbering down the hallway.

"T-bird! Reppin' the Lakeshow pretty hard."

"Got to."

You handle the steaks while your friends bro out. Broccoli is steaming in a pot. Terry moves into the living room to arrange the seating and fire up his pirated premium cable account. Todd walks up to you with genuine concern in his eyes and asks how you are coping and whether or not the government is providing any counseling. He almost regrets asking the question and just nods through the answer you both knew. You appreciate his concern, but you are eager to crack wise and share a meal with friends to get your mind off the situation. You decide against telling them about the conversation in the rose garden.

Todd sits in the corner of the dining nook as you start transferring the steaks and broccoli to plates.

"The milkman still delivers in K-town."

Bubbling with ferocity, Todd drags hard on the smoking apparatus until the entire tube is a milky, opaque white. He releases a dragon's plume out the south window. The smoke signal alerts the neighbors of impending heated philosophical discussions.

The three of you take up the white leather couch and saw away at the steaks as *America Primetime* host Dino Morland runs through the beats of his monologue. Donning a well-tailored black suit with a brown tie and pocket square, silver hair slicked back, Dino struts in front of the backdrop of a fictional city skyline. High production value fills the television screen as the glossy black floor shines and blue light bounces off the glass set pieces. The crowd claps through the final joke as Dino effortlessly segues.

"—but first, he is the governor of California, my old job, Garret Sturgis, ladies and gentlemen!"

A tall, slick man employing a strong pomade and looking suave in a grey suit slinks like a panther across the waxed floor and takes his seat across Dino.

"Garret, I have to commend you for being here, I know this is a very trying time for your administration."

"This is an extremely trying time for my administration, and more importantly for every citizen in Southern California, and to be quite candid the entire state and country as a whole. Let's be real Dino, with the current state of affairs you're lucky this program is still being beamed across the country; I mean, how many times did you lose internet bandwidth today? I've been in your green room trying to send an email for the last forty-five minutes."

"Yes, well, Chicken Little, I suppose you have a right to be dramatic considering the disaster that occurred ten days ago. How is your office managing the logistics of a recovery?"

"As best we can, Dino. We are providing food and water for every victim, but the cold fact is that we are more than two years into what is no longer a recession, but by definition a depression, and we need a drastic plan of action to fix our state and federal policies. Our federal government is failing us."

"To be fair, Garret, how about the millions and millions of dollars in tax revenue the state of California has crumpled into a ball and thrown out the proverbial window? This state has made it so difficult to run a profitable business on a large scale. We may be the prettiest girl at the dance, but the one who puts out is the one getting the limo to the afterparty."

The crowd erupts in laughter and cat calls as Dino smiles, smoothing his tie against his shirt.

"I kid, California, I kid, but seriously it looks like *Mad Max* out there. We had the nation's worst homeless problem before the disaster, what are you doing to solve this crisis?"

"This is true, a humanitarian tragedy has been unfolding in plain sight for the past half-decade. This has been a priority in the past for my predecessor, and remains a priority today for my administration. We continue to strive towards permanent housing, services and employment for our homeless citizens. Again, this comes down to a lack of federal funding. We can only stretch the California budget so far. The majority of the nation's homeless hop a Greyhound and come to our state. We need help. We can't even afford to pay our police officers and our firefighters. Where is FEMA right now? What have they done? Shipped people to live in giant tents in vacant lots across our neighboring states. We don't want this, we don't want to burden other states."

"How about these police officers and firefighters, and their unions, Garret. I agree that these brave men and women are crucial elements of society, but at what expense? It says here that in California eighteen of the top twenty overtime earning public workers were firefighters, and are you ready folks, they each brought in over four hundred thousand dollars a year. How many MREs and water bottles would that buy?"

"Dino, be realistic. Imagine a society without police officers and firefighters."

"Imagine your campaign without the union contributions."

The crowd lets loose a sustained gasp as Dino shifts in his chair and draws in a breath before collecting his thoughts, gesturing at Garret with an accusatory right hand.

"Do you think the system is broken, Garret? Do you think this information age is shining a harsh light on all of the bureaucracy and backroom handshakes, and the career politicians obviously out for their own self-interest?"

"I think you're reaching a little there, Dino, but I do agree with you that we have some serious fundamental problems with our government right now, which is why I am going keep fighting for my constituency."

"These are the jokes, ladies and gentlemen. Good luck Garret, thank you. Let's meet our next guests."

Garret slides off his chair and slips backstage while three new guests strut towards a rectangular black glass table. A snarky plump man in a shiny suit, a broad shouldered grump in a sportcoat, and a mousy woman with thick frames and a broad smile.

"He is the executive vice president of public relations at Duffy McLendon, please welcome Keith Duffy. Please welcome Lieutenant Colonel Weldon Whitlow, United States Army retired, and New York Times columnist and author Olivia Baker."

More applause from the crowd as Dino takes his seat and collects his buck slips and notecards.

"Let's start with you Keith, since your business is perception. Do you think this lingering recession is indeed a depression? What can companies do to get out of this bog and start turning a profit again?"

"They've been spending too much money on public relations," interrupts Lt. Col. Whitlow, to the delight of the crowd.

"Thank you, general. I can't comment on macroeconomics, but I can tell you from working with national corporations, times are tough across our entire country."

The mousy reporter from New York boldly interjects.

"I can comment on macroeconomics, considering I've written two books on the topic, and no Lt. Col., our corporations are not defaulting due to public relations expenditure. Let's start with our very own United States government. In 2017 we had over twenty trillion in debt. That is trillion with a T. Add all of the gold mined in one year to all of the worldwide oil exports in one year and you wouldn't be close. Combine the market capitalization of every single company in the S&P 500, you would not have twenty trillion. China had more debt than we did, and was exporting real estate bubbles across the world, look at Vancouver and Seattle. Don't even get me started on the failed experiment that was the European Union."

"How deep in the weeds are we going to get, Olivia? This is a comedy show."

"Give me a second. You asked. So we had an entire planet overextended and in debt, governments and citizens, and the financial sector continued to do exactly what they were doing during the 2007 financial crisis. They kept making bets via these exotic financial instruments that they themselves created. Look at the easy money policy courtesy of the Federal Reserve, European Central Bank, and Peoples Bank of China leading up to the 2017 bursting of a whole variety pack of artificially inflated bubbles. You know, when your 401k was cut in half."

Dino checks his notecard.

"Yes, it says here in January of 2017 banks in the United States had two hundred and forty-seven trillion dollars' worth of derivatives risk exposure."

"Exactly," continues Olivia, "and the banks' assets were in the billions, not trillions, so you can understand why that was a problem. Now to understand why we haven't recovered, acknowledge that the Federal Reserve and ECB can't just kick in a quantitative easing policy because they've already been doing it, and never stopped doing it these past thirteen years, and under this system they will never be able to stop doing it. Until they have run out of runway, that is, which is sooner than you'd think. So, yeah, we are in a depression, considering this has been going on for more than two years, and yeah, this is going to be worse than 1929, and no, we can't recover under these current conditions. The system is broken."

The audience is stunned. Every person in the studio knows that when they go shopping this week one dozen eggs will cost double the usual price, but they were not prepared to hear that this was going to be the case for an extended period of time, and according to this economic journalist, it was going to get worse.

Whitlock clears his throat and pipes up.

"Yes. I agree with the statements Olivia just made. You can disagree if you like, but there is no denying that we can't pay our bills, and this seems to be a worldwide issue. Now, I want to talk about how this situation is giving us a real shot in the shorts. I don't think I'm letting the cat out of the bag here, but our military has been shrinking, and not because we worked our way to world peace, but because we can't pay our own soldiers. The U.S. armed forces are on a skeleton crew. Let's take California for example. We have the Baja epidemic in San Diego. The remaining naval units that aren't under mandatory quarantine are responsible for protecting the entire western half of our country and our allies. In 2012 we had eight deployed aircraft carriers protecting our way of life. Now we have three, two in the Mediterranean for our friends in the Middle East and one WESTPAC deployment. Do you think this is a coincidence? We can protect the nuclear armaments in Seal Beach and maybe one or two major cities. You didn't think it was strange when those Chinese frigates took an unescorted tour of Northern California last month? Everyone here knows about the Russian aircraft sightings."

Olivia pours gasoline on the fire.

"The financial sector ran amok and destroyed the consumer. Without the consumer the companies defaulted. Without the companies the jobs disappeared. No jobs means no tax revenue. Ask yourselves in the audience, out of ten friends how many are paying taxes right now? How many are working?"

Keith Duffy has been wearing a slack jawed grimace for the last nine minutes. Dino bounces the edge of his notecards off the glass table.

"I was going to ask the panel about social security and healthcare, but I can see the pitchforks in the audience. We're going to bring out actor and director Ryan Russell Dunaway!"

"So he can tell us about a bankrupt LAPD and how he and his Hollywood cronies employ paramilitary private security forces to protect their homes and studio backlots," chimes Lt. Col. Whitlock.

The screen goes black as Terry holds the remote in his hand, tossing it back on the table. A perturbed Todd traipses into the kitchen and sets the burner to a pot of filtered water, producing from his backpack a mason jar of freshly ground Guatemalan Coban Santa Isabel, custom filters, and a pour-over dripper system, all courtesy of Blue Bottle Coffee.

The three of you harmonize a collective sigh. You're all old enough to remember a childhood in the '90s, before the backspin of a basketball was replaced with the glow of a connected device. You pity the youth of today, and feel a sick sense of gratitude that you were able to experience what may have been the peak of history's greatest documented empire. The books mark 9/11 as the defining turning point in your portion of late modernity, but wisdom dictates the financial system has always been the most potent terrorist.

Notes of apricot, marjoram, and boysenberry do their best to cut through the sense of pervasive hopelessness. As you enjoy your coffee Terry seems to collect himself to speak.

"Look, and this is aimed more towards you, not Johnny Smokestack over there, but I've been bouncing something around in my head and this feels like the time to share it."

Terry leafs through a few of the bound presentation materials he has stacked up beside his coffee table, opening the pages portraying various manners of philanthropy, renewable energies, and community outreach.

"You know what my company is all about, right? You know what type of person Peter Triton is. I play hoops with the CFO at Los Amigos Park every Tuesday night. Dude loves me. Obviously he's got Triton's ear, and the last few months he keeps dropping these hints that something is going down. He's trying to recruit me up to Triton's property in Montecito so they can vet me, include me in whatever righteous endeavor is in motion. He won't say what, I don't even think he knows what, but even though the dollar has gone to dirt Triton still has the billions to make a difference. I've known you for a decade, I know what you bring to the table. I can vouch for you."

Todd kisses his left set of knuckles.

"Call me Johnny Smokestack again, city boi. Seriously though, I'm heading up to the Emerald Triangle for a few weeks; it's on my way, you can skip the train."

Terry tosses the presentations back on the coffee table.

"You have that look in your eye like you're dying to contribute and you don't know how. I've got my job, I can help people in my own way. Todd is permeating health and keeping people sane. What are you going to do, keep screaming yourself awake every night?"

Caffeine adds to the rush as your mind flips through the scenes of the day and an obvious opportunity to be a positive force in the universe. Terry looks at you.

II
Earth

1

You would have enjoyed riding the spine of the Pacific Coast Highway and tipping your cap to Malibu and the glittering blue expanse that sits west of California State Route 1. This was not in the cards considering the proximity of a much uglier cousin: U.S. Route 101. Two miles north of Koreatown, via Normandie Ave, Todd's Cosmic Grey Pearl 2009 Honda Civic hums its wheels onto the 101 north on-ramp.

Traversing the Hollywood Hills, and then the San Fernando Valley, you and the 101 are making short work of Los Angeles County. One of the original national routes established in 1926, the old grey snake has borne many a passenger on its back, and has been privy to more than a few tire shredding, spark flying, watch out for that ricocheted 9 mm, crumple zone crushing, air bag deploying, spike strip enhanced, gang sign flashing, PIT maneuvering, high speed and low speed police pursuits; one look at the tar striped lanes, cracked pavement, skid marks, scraped concrete walls, random errant hubcaps, and glass dusted shoulders can attest.

As usual, the sun is shining on this fine October morning, and the interior of Todd's car warms the bones while a crisp rush of cool air sneaks from the air conditioning vents. Your duffel bag is in the trunk, packed with some clean clothing, your Smith and Wesson with ammunition, the butterfly knife, your passport, some bottles of water, and a paperback edition of Edward Bunker's *No Beast So Fierce*, borrowed from Terry. You don't have a phone, and the vehicle lacks Bluetooth, so you and Todd are enjoying the brand of lively conversation you usually share, with Todd focusing on the positivity of your cloudy objective and his own plans to visit the Bristlecone Pines in the White Mountains of California, five thousand year old trees that he believes will provide inspiration and direction simply by their presence.

North of the Santa Monica Mountains the 101 travels west, through Thousand Oaks, Camarillo, and Ventura before hitting the edge of the earth at Emma Wood State Beach, and bordering the planet's largest and deepest ocean basin for the twenty-five miles to Santa Barbara County. There is a distinct lack of vegetation up to a certain level on the slopes of the passing hills. Your window is down now and the salt water moisture is evaporating on your skin. The rocky brown bluffs to your right remind you faintly of Santa Monica, but you are so obviously out of Los Angeles you can feel it. The weight that any hustling, bustling city drives down against a person's shoulders has been lifted and you feel optimistic staring past the white sea spray and into the infinite blue horizon.

Following the instructions Terry scribbled in his hieroglyphic penmanship, you exit north onto San Ysidro Rd. You are officially in Montecito, Santa Barbara County, where there are more trees than people, and the abundance of oxygen is obvious in comparison to the home of the scandalous, smog choked Los Angeles. The tsunami waves were not as catastrophic for south facing Santa Barbara County, and half a mile up San Ysidro you see no signs of previous inundation. These are not homes, these are estates, and each property is more impressive as you continue north on San Ysidro, and east on Sinaloa Dr, as Todd pretends to do a bump off his right wrist. A few hundred feet across Sinaloa and Todd slows to a gravelly stop on the shoulder of Maria Del Carmen Dr. Standing in the gravel and dust you embrace your friend and shake Todd's hand.

"Until that day, compadre."

"Until that day."

The Civic kicks up dirt as you place your duffel bag against a tree and examine your surroundings. Maria Del Carmen is off the beaten path, and you are definitely standing amongst the ultra-wealthy. There is absolutely no traffic and the only source of sound is a Northern Mockingbird stringing together a medley of his greatest hits. One estate directly in front of you takes up what would constitute a city block. To your left is a walled off compound and to your right is a long row of trees acting as a natural barrier for what looks like a farm.

Fifteen minutes later a man with a closely cropped haircut and a gold buttoned blue blazer appears from between two trees lining the grasslands. He is piloting a red Garia Monaco luxury golf cart with walnut leather seats and black rims. Stopping in front of you he monotonously delivers:

"He... is actually six-five."

"With the afro, six-nine," you reply with a knowing smile as you sling the duffel into the rear storage and take the passenger seat.

Whipping around at a surprising speed, you're forced to grab the metal guard beside your seat as the vehicle splits the row of trees and begins spanning the property.

"This isn't exactly street legal. They only sell this model in Europe. Do you like Faith No More?"

You are shocked when the man who has not introduced himself produces an honest to God compact disc from the rear compartment and slips Faith No More's *The Real Thing* into the on-board media system.

Traveling at least twenty-five miles per hour, you are eating up acres of property that resemble unutilized farmland. Towards the end of this untilled field you see a narrow white bridge leading across a moat and dead ending into rainforest grade shrubbery. You feel enough of the bass drum that you suspect this golf cart is hiding some brand of miniature subwoofer.

The unidentified man has not eased one pascal of penny loafer pressure on the accelerator pedal as you hit a narrow white bridge barely wide enough to accommodate the Monaco. The terrain change from soil to wooden bridge bucks both back tires six inches off the ground, lurching the rear to the left while the front half of the cart skids to the right, sending smooth black stones airborne. Leaning half way out of the cart and wrenching the wheel to the left he pilots directly into the wall of oakleaf hydrangea.

Exploding through the foliage, you have entered immaculately maintained garden grounds sprawling before an awe-inspiring manor. The Monaco carves to the right and digs into the lush grass, leaving a sickle shaped groove as the cart comes to rest on the bank of a pond.

"Hang loose, rook."

The man has positioned his gyrating wrist in front of his face. As his cuff recedes to his elbow, he barks:

"Hit track three!"

Fishing two Kona Big Wave Golden Ales out of the dashboard cooler he uses the flesh of his forearm to twist and pop the bottle caps. Shoving one beer into your hands, he begins whipping his right arm in a fly fishing motion and swaying his torso back and forth in unison with the third track intro.

"Bassline of the decade."

As you witness this performance, your eyes are drawn to the seven hundred feet of lush garden grounds, leading to a formal three tiered English landscape garden before a four section three storied manor. There are more windows than you can count while sitting in a rocking luxury golf cart.

"I know, this place is sick. Triton isn't here. This portion of the op concludes in less than twenty-four hours. You'll be speaking with Mallory in a few minutes. You like the beer?"

"Excellent beer."

You both sit without speaking as the man nods with the bass and fires off a straight right hand with each strike of the snare drum. Suddenly he twists down the volume nob and presses his palm against his left ear, smiling:

"I know you can see me, that's your job. Maybe the last one... yeah. You wouldn't be doing that if the big man was here. Ha, an ape with good taste!"

The man guzzles the remaining half of his beer.

"Roger."

Collecting himself, he looks in your direction and dips his head in a single nod. Turning forward he begins piloting the Monaco towards the manor at a very reasonable speed. He extends a callused right paw:

"Jeffrey."

2

Arriving at the formal gardens you are greeted by two older, gaunt men with thin lipped coin slot snarls and an air of superiority.

"Alarming punctuality, Jeffrey. Thankfully we heard your usual serenade from one thousand feet."

Shuffling towards you with their grey slacks, black overcoats, and white vests one of the servants grabs your duffel bag as the other leads you up the tiers of the English landscape garden.

"Hope to see you later, rookie," exclaims Jeffrey prior to his jolting departure across the grounds.

You are led up white stairs and onto a patio with white cushioned furniture to your left, to your right are metal frames of more patio furniture lacking cushions that must be off somewhere being vacuumed and wiped down. Directly behind you and situated above the stairs, facing the manor, is a twenty by ten foot diorite sculpture in a rounded shape representing a reclining woman.

"The master enjoys the igneous variety. Here we are."

Each taking the handle of one of the corresponding immense French doors, the servants open them in unison and gesture for you to enter. You step into the great hall of this substantial mansion, turning for a moment to take in the astounding view spreading out beyond the sculpture. Each one of your footsteps echoes off the intricate designs that comprise the marble mosaic floor. The open floorplan is devoid of much furniture, save a random gilded desk, and there are marble busts on pedestals placed before black marble columns leading up towards a white cathedral ceiling.

Steered down a hallway, you enter an elegant drawing room. At the opposite end of the room is a crackling fireplace. Before you is the back of a U shaped dark moss green suede couch, placed on a fine Soumak rug resting on the room's tigerwood flooring. There is an array of chairs and end tables placed about the room, some topped by miniature volumes of black leather bound books and platinum framed portraits. White roses adorn the end tables, and parts of the mantle not occupied by larger, more ornate paintings. Cozy.

You are examining the miniature books on the U shaped jade desk surrounding the couch when a serpentine hand appears across the back cushion. A lounging woman is in the process of sitting upright, she turns her head and smiles. Standing and walking around the furniture she is wearing a black dress with shoulder pads and a deeply plunging neckline. Dark brown hair thick and parted from one side, manicured eyebrows, knowing eyes that appear almost black, ruby red lips glossed and curled into a wry smile, and an extremely healthy bust of porcelain meat. As you're looking at the shimmering peek of a black silk bra you take note of the large diamond necklace of a circle within a circle, and the dangling diamond earrings. She is standing before you now with her hand outstretched.

"Pleased to meet you, my name is Mallory. Your timing is impeccable. You are the last person I am going to interview before we move along. Please take a seat wherever you like. Water? Espresso? Champagne," she says with a cheeping laugh.

Accepting the offer of espresso you seat yourself in a plush moss green suede chair. Mallory sits across from you.

"Now, someone with an opinion that Gordon seems to admire came forth and vouched for you, and Gordon phoned me; so that is why you are here, but why are you here?"

"I was on the coast of Venice when the tsunami wiped out a chunk of Los Angeles. I have no home, no car, no job, and almost no possessions. I am healthy, athletic, intelligent, capable, motivated, hardworking, and looking to contribute. I take this situation very seriously as this may be my only opportunity to be a source of light in a quickly dimming world. There is that voice in the back of our head that all of us hear and few of us heed, I follow my moral compass because I learned at a young age when you do evil it comes back to you, and when you do good it seems to return at a greater level than you put out. I am trying to survive."

"My dear, Gordon didn't tell me you were there. Bless you. Do you love your country?"

"Yes."

"Identify for me the three most serious problems that exist in this country today."

"The dissolved family structure. Income inequality, and a wildly irresponsible, broken financial system. A lack of respect and tolerance. The choice of endless hours of mindless entertainment above culture. A lackadaisical, unconstructively critical, close minded, and polarized populace. A failing education system."

"You can count to three, yes?"

"Shall I go on?"

One of the servants presents you with an intricately carved silver tray transporting a double shot of crema topped espresso.

"Just checking. Lastly, are you prepared to do what it takes to promote our common good?"

"Absolutely."

"This has been enlightening. As I mentioned, we are towards the end of this process here and the house is quite empty. Normally we might have a dinner, but I have numerous loose ends to attend to before we ship out tomorrow morning. This evening I will be on the satellite phone with Peter discussing, among other things, my impression of you and your possible fit on our little team."

Mallory stands up and walks over to a gilded desk supporting her Hermès Shiny Porosus Crocodile Birkin 35 Bleu Abysse. Rifling through the bag you hear the clinking of heavy metals until she pulls out a thick red key with the letters S F and a black horse prancing before a yellow emblem. She tosses it in your direction.

"So, tell you what. You've had a rough go of things, why don't you take Peter's car through downtown and enjoy dinner on me."

She hands you a crumpled wad of five one hundred-dollar bills.

"It does not go without saying, so I'm going to say it to you; that car has a tracking device, and if you do anything stupid like drive to San Francisco, I'll make sure you catch a .30-06 in the chest, or maybe a serrated KA-BAR in the base of the skull if I'm having a bad day. The servants will show you to your room when you return. Enjoy. Oh, you can drive a stick, yes?"

"Definitely."

3

Minutes later you and the head butler are standing in a garage resembling more of an aircraft hangar than a carport. There are eleven covered vehicles parked in a geometrically perfect row formation.

"This has more square footage than my old apartment building."

"Which of the keys did the Lady give you?"

You show him the key and a smug laugh escapes another coin slot mouth as the butler rolls his eyes and walks over to the third vehicle, ripping the cover off in a histrionic reveal.

"This is a 1967 Ferrari P3/4. This vehicle raced, and wrecked, in the 1966 and 1967 24 Hours of Le Mans. Painstakingly restored with the blessing of the legendary Enzo Ferrari, this masterpiece now finds itself under the custodianship of Peter Triton."

The bubbly and curvaceous work of art resembles a Ford GT40 Mark II, only painted Ferrari red with a voluptuous styling like the GT spent the summer eating pasta and doing two cycles of anabolic steroids. This is without a doubt the most beautiful, captivating machine you will ever see. The high arching lines of the front end curve towards a smooth glass cockpit and duck into induction vents on the sides of a meaty back end; a gleaming deep-red rocket ship styled in two waves. On the doors, and below the wide induction at the center of the hood, large white circular emblems display the black faced and tea rose orange bordered number twenty-three.

"We have a fondness for prime numbers around here. Please mind your head."

Taking a lap around the machine you see a spare racing tire beneath the spoiler, PROVA MO-36 painted in white next to the tire, and a ferocious set of quadruple exhaust pipes. As the butler lifts the suicide door you notice the Ferrari prancing horse emblem below the rear view mirror, a Fram Filters decal, a Prestone Performance decal, and a Champion Spark Plugs decal along the door. You laugh as you climb in via the left side door and notice you have to climb over to the right side steering wheel.

"This vehicle weighs sixteen hundred pounds with four hundred twenty horsepower courtesy of a twelve cylinder engine. Capable of a top speed exceeding one hundred eighty-six miles per hour, I strongly suggest you pay mind to that back end, considering the preposterous power to weight ratio."

Strapping yourself to the red leather bucket seats via racing harness, you notice the interior is completely bare bones save a wheel, a few switches, and an instrument displaying speed, revolutions per minute, and temperature. You don't tell the butler that operating the manual shift with your left hand is going to take some getting used to. Stomping your foot on the clutch you pump the accelerator a few times and flick the ignition switch. A rasping explosion roars from the rear of the vehicle.

"Hoooooly sh—"

A stomp of the accelerator sends the guttural roar into a screaming burst of increased pitch. You ease off the clutch, then smooth back down and tap the accelerator as the wheels start to push forward under threat of a potential rear engine torque explosion. With an ear to ear grin you salute the concerned butler and start to navigate the circular European style driveway. As you are rounding the large fountain you can hear and see Jeffrey rocking out in his Garia Monaco. He has ceased his frantic movement and sits in a stupefied state of amazement. Sidling up to his position you hover your foot over the accelerator as the exhaust rumbles, deep and menacing.

"This isn't exactly street legal."

Jeffrey rifles both his fisted arms upward in a triumphant vertical display of respect as you slam the accelerator and fishtail briefly before fading down the distance of the main driveway in a symphony of fuel injected eruptions.

Turning a few heads on E Valley Rd, you corner left on the now familiar straightaway that is San Ysidro Rd. Leaves are ripped from trees and shrubbed impediments as it takes you thirty-six seconds of cacophonous howling to cover the one mile south back to the 101. One minute and forty-five seconds on the 101 north, as you ruin a few backstrokes at the

Montecito Country Club, you take the Garden St exit and merge onto State St at a safe and respectable speed. After all, you are not an animal.

The afternoon climate is especially agreeable as a draught wafts in through the open roof of this spyder convertible. The Plexiglas driver and passenger windows are riveted in place and there is no window in the rear. You are pleased with the aerodynamics. Growling along the two lane street you take in the terracotta tile rooves and white walled Spanish stylings of the one story bars, restaurants, bookstores, lounges, and coffee shops. You cruise by Hotel Santa Barbara, noticing it is one of the few buildings on this main drag that exceeds two stories. Scantily clad young adults and individuals in their late teens savvy enough to have acquired fake identification whoop it up at the cantina. A relaxed, celebratory vibe permeates the atmosphere. What a far cry from the death and destruction that will always haunt you. You shake your head at the high sequel numbers beside every film playing at the Metro 4 Theater. There is the ubiquitous poster for the upcoming *Metal Dude 9*. Everyone is smiling and chatting while toting shopping bags through the outdoor shops and restaurants that incorporate the Paseo Nuevo. Towards the north end of State St towers the Granada Theater. Standing at eight stories and boasting fifteen hundred seats within an opulent, gilded interior, the local landmark has provided a century worth of culture; you notice the marquee advertising the Santa Barbara Symphony's performance of Vivaldi's *The Four Seasons*.

Your mind registers a slight self-conscious twinge as the car continues to produce a racket that sounds like fifteen rubber hammers banging around the inside of a commercial grade dryer. This feeling is easily overpowered by the pure joy of piloting this automobile. E Sola St marks the end of commercial downtown Santa Barbara, and you continue north on State St, beginning to contemplate dinner options. After half a mile you intersect with Mission St. Immediately you think of visiting Fr. Virgil at the famed Mission Santa Barbara. Arriving in this opulence and presenting yourself to a man who took a vow of poverty seems exceptionally gauche, yet Fr. Virgil seemed to understand you to your core, and you can park the Ferrari at the back corner of the lot. Following the signs you travel east on Mission and north on Laguna St, parking your vintage prototype Ferrari under the shadow of a Lincoln Navigator in the southwestern corner of the lot.

You inelegantly shift out of the racing style seats and yank yourself from the cockpit. Walking towards the church compound you are floored by the serendipity of life. A short time ago you were a homeless Los Angeleno, sitting in a rose garden, benefiting from the wise counsel of a Franciscan; now you've just wrenched yourself out of an eight figure automobile, and find yourself walking through an even larger and more impressive nineteen plot Mission Rose Garden, seeking counsel from that same priest.

The Mission Santa Barbara is a Spanish mission founded by the Franciscan order in 1786 on the feast day of Saint Barbara. The objective was to convert the indigenous

Chumash Barbareño tribe of Native Americans. The grounds are extensive and you are walking across the black topped plaza. The pavement still carries hints of faint pastel outlines from the vibrant, large scale images left by Madonnari Festival street painters. The chapel is built with native yellow sandstone held together by lime made from seashells. This is the only mission with two identical bell towers. They each stand eighty-seven feet tall and twenty feet square. Climbing the steps of the chapel you enter through the colossal wooden doors.

The chapel proves why this mission is known as "Queen of the Missions." Built in classic Greco-Roman design, the graceful earth toned beauty of the forty-two foot walls are painted with garlands. The ceiling and flooring are original, as are the winged tongues of lightning based on a 27 B.C. design by Roman architect Marcus Vitruvius Pollio. The entire chapel is copied from the Roman's designs, as his work *The Six Books of Architecture* can be found in the Mission archives. One hundred sixty-two feet long and twenty-seven feet wide, the walls are six feet thick with nine foot square stone buttresses. You are facing the abalone-encrusted Chumash altar dating back to the 1790s. Hanging on the left wall is a nine by fourteen foot painting representing the assumption and coronation of the Virgin Mary, on the right wall hangs a painting of equal size depicting the Crucifixion. A sight to behold, and California Historical Landmark No. 309, you wet your fingers with holy water and touch your forehead, chest, and shoulders. You sit alone for a moment on one of the wooden pews, until a woman enters from an adjoining chamber. You rise and walk towards her.

"Excuse me, is Fr. Virgil here?"

"Yes, but you'll have to donate for a self-guided tour to visit that section of the grounds."

"Wait, what?"

"He rests in the mausoleum at the center of the Historic Cemetery."

Your mind works on the logic of the situation.

"When did he pass?"

"It was... May of 2008, sweetheart."

She points to where you can receive the materials for a self-guided tour, then walks the length of the chapel, entering another chamber behind the altar as you try and balance yourself on the back of a pew. You're wobbling in disbelief and looking at the large crucifix below the ceiling, and then staring at the Lamb of God on the altar, feeling confused, betrayed, and afraid. You shuffle towards the exit and push through the wooden doors, nearly collapsing on the steps, sitting again with your head in your hands.

Trying to make sense of the situation might be too difficult in your current mental state, so you focus on why you feel the way you do. Fear is not the correct emotion. No one has betrayed you. That was only positivity. Your heartbeat is slowing from the frantic pulse moments ago, and the cold sweat is drying on your skin. You walk back into the chapel and find your way to the office. You palm the wad of money Mallory gave you for dinner and place it as a donation to improve the garden, enhance the museum, and most importantly, contribute to the Virgil Cordano Living Memory Fund. As you exit through the chapel you place your hand in the holy water and make the sign of the cross.

No one visits as you sit in silence for an hour on the large field near the Mission Rose Garden. Your mind is relatively blank as you attempt to process your emotions. Feeling the urge to move, you squeeze into the Ferrari. It feels good to have no stereo, hence no music but the thunder of the engine, the wind streaming across the cockpit, and the thoughts turning in your mind.

Blazing by the Mission, Los Olivos St becomes Mission Canyon Rd. You're gaining altitude. Foothill Rd by the Tennis Club of Santa Barbara, you're heading east until you hit Mountain Dr, veering left onto Gibraltar Rd. Altitude is gaining fast, from this mountain road you can see three miles to the ocean. You are rising while the sun is falling. Understanding what the butler said about power to weight ratio, the torque is unreal as it whips the back end of this hurtling masterpiece, sliding through every turn, eating asphalt at high decibels. The royal blue sky gives way to cyan, before dissolving to layers of thistle, apricot, and vermilion.

You leave the racecar on a dirt shoulder and hike two minutes to sit on the top of Gibraltar Rock. You're looking across Rattlesnake Canyon, you're almost in line with La Cumbre Peak, the three thousand nine hundred ninety-seven foot peak in the Santa Ynez Mountains. Four thousand feet in the sky and five miles from the ocean, the city of Santa Barbara twinkles below you. Your insignificance and your grandeur have never been so simultaneously evident. The celestial pastels from minutes prior are now in the process of being swallowed by black. You decide they will soon be expecting you in Montecito, and you'd rather not get carjacked and stomach a blade from one of the Goleta gang members that come up here at night to drink forty ounce cervezas.

Carving down the mountain your reflexes ease your trajectory when the headlights catch two California mule deer trotting down Gibraltar Rd. A doe and her juvenile offspring gracefully veer to the right and fearlessly leap over the brush, seemingly off the side of the mountain, yet you know they are deftly descending as they seek refuge from interlopers.

The cockpit of the P3/4 is approaching ninety-nine degrees despite the invigorating instants chilled night air sneaks over the windshield. You are less adamant with the accelerator on the return ride. Coasting down the thousand feet of driveway, you idle in front of the garage while a new blue blazer man dismounts a generic cream E-Z-GO golf cart and fingers a keypad. The blazer man readjusts your parking job so the vehicles are again in their perfect row, and you see him covering the vehicle as you enter the main residence. A servant is standing in one of the halls to escort you to your bedroom. Before he does so he hands you a folded piece of paper the size of a greeting card. The texture is rough like papyrus.

"Congratulations, you have a seat at the table. Get your rest. Breakfast will be served in your room at 8 a.m. Be prepared to depart promptly at 9 a.m. -M"

You are led to a bedroom on the third floor of an eerily silent wing. The room is decorated in a similar fashion to the drawing room. Your duffel bag rests on a jade ottoman in front of an elegant wood carved bed. Resting on the bed are three sets of fatigues with black and brown camouflage that somehow seems like it was designed with an artist's touch. There is a logo on the left breast of a T with a trident spearing from the top of the letter.

Placing the fatigues on the nightstand you turn down the covers and stare at the ceiling before using the pull chain on the lamp.

4

Poached eggs, strawberries, thick cuts of bacon, and the richest espresso you've enjoyed, off another finely crafted silver tray. The room is warm and toasty due to a low burning fire, one you did not light. Sneaky servants. You shower and dress in the fatigues, sending phantom compliments to whoever eyeballed your size. Shouldering the duffle bag you walk out of the room suspecting you won't be experiencing that level of comfort for some time.

Jeffrey is standing in the courtyard next to the main driveway, dressed in the same style of fatigues with a rucksack at his feet.

"Top of the morning, tenderfoot! That was some sled you got to push around, huh?"

A black on black Mercedes G65 AMG with limo tint drifts to a stop near the driveway fountain. Jeffrey opens up the rear passenger door and slides to the driver side of the back seat, then leans back towards the open door and gestures to the rucksack he left on the ground. You throw his rucksack and your duffel bag into the trunk and take your seat on the rear passenger side. Jeffrey slaps the driver on the shoulder.

"Morning, Smitty."

The man at the wheel is wearing a black sportcoat, black tie, and black driver's cap. He nods to Jeffrey. The vehicle begins to coast around the fountain as you ask your travelling companion:

"Is Mallory coming?"

"Psh."

Looking out the window you methodically hash over the surreal stream of events that have taken course. Marvelous California terrain soars by your window as the SUV transitions from the 101 to the 154 west, and before long you are cutting through Los Padres National Forest. With just the hum of all-terrain tires spinning on freeway you turn to Jeffrey.

"Do you know what we're planning on doing?"

"No. I can tell you where we're going though. We are en route to a ranch west of the 101 and east of Big Sur. More like a compound Triton has set up. There's even a winery, but that's kind of a front. This place is massive, you'll like it."

"How long have you been with Triton?"

Jeffrey laughs and places his foot on the center console, to the dismay of the driver.

"Look, rook, you impressed me with that burnout. It made me feel like the human spirit is still alive. We have a bit of a car ride ahead of us, so I'll spin you a damn yarn, but don't go telling people I said I liked your style. You can probably tell by looking at me I've got some military experience. I've been involved in some ops you've probably heard of, I've been involved in some ops you definitely don't know about, and I've been some places you definitely don't know we've been; and don't ask, I respect the code. When I was a young lad the United States Marine Corps took it upon themselves to make me an expert in a tube-launched, optically tracked, wire-guided anti-tank missile system. I was what they call a TOW Gunner. Now I'm sure you heard about that little Black Hawk helicopter incident the army had in 1993. What most people don't know—and not like it's classified, it isn't—is that a year before that incident me and eighteen hundred of my closest friends stormed Mogadishu so that aid workers could safely feed those starving Somalians. You see, I was the tip of the spear. A bullet catcher. A lot of people don't remember that the Italians were there, the British and Portuguese, and I got a nice close look at how the war machine works. After proving myself in Somalia, someone suggested I join a Force Reconnaissance company, and I will tell you from experience that Force Recon makes a young man grow up quick, and grow up strong. They served up a steady dose of direct action ops and I continued to display my charming personality. I closed out my career as a high level deep reconnaissance operative. I'm talkin' deep, like your mother's—"

Horns blare as Smitty attempts to change lanes without checking his blind spot.

"Come on, Smitty! You had one job! One job, I says. Anyway, I've been some places, seen some things. I've been all over Africa, the Middle East, I've terrorized the Four Floors of Whores, and I've even scuba-dived off Phuket. To this day, almost thirty years later, I hear they still won't let Marines take R&R there, after what we did. They used to call me the Tequila Werewolf, and I've punched out my fair share of cops."

"That's pretty intense, Jeffrey. I didn't get that vibe when we were having a beer."

"Yeah, well I've mellowed out in my old age. I spent a lot of time in the brig, singing Alice In Chains. I spent a few years in San Diego at the bottom of a bottle, playing disc golf at the world renowned Morley Field. That's when a nice little Guamanian I was shacked with informed me that Peter Triton was recruiting a special security detail, one to watch his six while he expanded some of his businesses internationally, reaching out to some of the more dicey corners of the world. The work was fulfilling, the pay was nice, and Pete and I really hit it off. These days I avoid the liquor and stick to beer, and I've been with Pete for close to a decade. I'm actually one of the people that vetted the candidates for this endeavor."

"You don't know exactly what we're doing, but you know who is going to be there. What type of people did you accept?"

"Well, it's a combination of retired military, or people the military couldn't afford, and some people that excel in logistics, you've got a few people from this little club Peter is a part of, you've got some computer guys, and you've got intangibles like yourself."

You decide to leave the conversation where it is, nodding and turning back to the window. This situation is increasingly intense, but you maintain this is the best, and honestly only, option. If this all ends in a ring of fire you want to know you went down swinging, in the light, trying to save your country from itself. You notice out the window you are in what people call "wine country."

"Rook. I'll tell you what you want to know."

"What's that?"

"What it's like to kill someone."

"Uh."

"Imagine you're standing in a large square room with white walls, a white ceiling, white floors and no furniture. Walk up to the center of the room. There is a thick red line painted across the floor from wall to wall. Not a thin line, a thick line. You are standing there, toeing the line, and a voice fills the room. The voice says you know this is wrong. The voice says people sacrificed so you could be in this room, people spent their own time on someone else so that you could be who you are, standing right here. This is not who you are. Then you step one foot over that line, and bring your other foot right next to that step, and it feels terrible. You know you made a mistake, and you know you can't step back; but the longer you stand there, the less it hurts."

The valley is covered in brown grass between rolling olive green hills, raw umber mountains in the near distance, rows of vibrant grape vines saturate the landscape. The SUV travels down a dirt road towards the foothills, you see the white wooden beams characteristic of California ranch fencing. You travel under a twenty foot tall ranch sign lording over the road, it displays only the symbol of a trident.

"That's why I'm here. I'm done killing. I want to stop the hate, stop the corruption, and I'll do it any way I can, just not by killing anyone."

5

Bumping along the dirt road your SUV curls around a foothill and the true nature of this ranch is blatantly apparent. The quaint ranch sign is some manner of ruse or diversion. Square miles have been carved into a secluded portion of these mountains. This flatland nestled between foothills is completely hidden from any town or highway. Dozens of colonial buildings stretch beyond your field of view. Some are arranged in a hexagonal formation, facing each other with well-manicured parade grounds between them. Others are in rows, one has five helipads beside the building, with two helipads occupied by matte black AugustaWestland AW101 twenty-four passenger helicopters. One of the helicopters has a general purpose machine gun and four large missiles.

"Those are MARTE anti-ship missiles," explains Jeffrey.

The SUV arrives at the ten foot tall fence that spans foothill to foothill. Surveillance cameras and razor wire. Three guards clutch bullpup combat rifles and maintain their alert status, while one of them walks to the vehicle and gives Jeffrey an elaborate series of fist bumps. The gate draws open and your vehicle continues along a bridge, crossing a large ditch dug behind the fencing.

"BMCRs from TX Ballistics, a Malaysian company. Triton does a fair amount of business in that region of Asia, it's pretty easy to sneak a few combat rifles into a shipping container undetected. Chambered for 5.56 NATO rounds, but they use the 7.62 for that adios power in case anyone wants to ruin the fiesta. Full auto."

Hypnotized by the divergence of man-made landscape and the picturesque mountain backdrop, your attention is held until your view is interrupted by eight legitimate artillery pieces in a perfect row formation.

"You just gave me a speech about improving our way of life without killing anyone!"

"I am, and Peter knows it. You haven't heard the plan, and I haven't heard the plan. Have some faith and get situated. Patience, grasshopper. Those are M777 Lightweight Towed Howitzers. State of the art towed artillery piece, 155mm and almost half the weight of the M198 it replaced. Mammoth Mountain actually uses a WWII era M114 Howitzer to bust up the packed snow to ensure skiers and those infernal snowboarders don't have to eat an avalanche."

Jeffrey reaches into his shoulder pocket and removes a pack of Winston cigarettes. Rolling down the window, with the scrape of a flint orange light bounces off his face, he drags a relaxed puff.

"You see, rook, America passed the National Firearms Act in 1934. To this day someone can go through an FBI interview and a background check, maybe some ATF red tape, and that person can buy all sorts of items classified as a 'destructive device.' The government is supposed to withhold one critical element of the device, but they usually forget, and if they remember we can go on an auction site to complete the puzzle. We have ourselves an entire brigade on this base right now. That means fifteen hundred people split into three battalions, five hundred people in each battalion. It only takes a handful of people to go through the proper paperwork, and maybe visit a few different states, and then a captain of industry comes by with a flatbed or a semi and here we are."

This ranch, which you now refer to as a base, is much larger than it appeared at the fence. Throughout your slow crawl across the grounds you have witnessed a colony of black and brown fatigues hurrying about this hidden realm. Jeffrey has not exaggerated in regards to manpower, or womanpower for that matter.

"Barracks four, Smitty. Thanks. See, there's one of the vineyards."

Roughly twenty rows of vines stretch across a portion of hill that appears to enjoy an abundance of sunshine.

"That's Cabernet right there, about one thousand vines. We've got Merlot, Pinot Noir—I'm sure you'll be pleased, you seem like someone that enjoys curling up with a crisp Chardonnay—we've got that too. Ah, here we are."

The collection of buildings that comprise the barracks structures resemble an Ivy League university campus more than housing for a paramilitary force. There are a series of people wearing service uniforms and not fatigues, carrying sheets, pillows, and towels out of the doors. This man is preaching equality, yet here is the servant class tending to his faithful. You justify this by acknowledging that Triton is providing these individuals with jobs, and you are planning on reserving judgement until your much anticipated briefing. The SUV rolls to a stop beside barracks four. Jeffrey hops out of the vehicle:

"Dismount. Handle those bags, rookie!"

"Handle your own bag, psycho."

"Bucking for promotion! I like the initiative," Jeffrey bellows as he slaps his stomach. Shouldering his own rucksack, you both proceed into the building.

Upon entrance Jeffrey slaps a clipboard out of the hands of a spindly young man, which you pick up and return. Jeffrey lumbers up the nearest flight of stairs. The man looks at you and runs a finger down the clipboard.

"Thank you. You are in room two eleven."

Running your hands along a smooth and polished wooden banister you climb the stairs and arrive at your second floor room. In the running theme of Triton décor, everything is exquisitely luxurious. The three corners away from the entrance have been divided into lodging areas, divided by floor to ceiling tapestries. Each "bunk" includes a complexly carved full sized bed, an antique Martin Maier flat top oak trunk serving as footlocker, a miniature refrigerator, waste bin, and a carved crown and gated top mahogany desk riddled with storage compartments and pigeonholes, dovetailed by hand.

In the bunk directly in front of you reclines an unremarkable man in his thirties. He is reading *Library of Apollodorus of Athens, the Grammarian*, which he lowers upon your entrance.

"Fresh fish! Welcome. That's you in the southwest corner. That's Catherine, and right there is Grommet."

A stunning statuesque woman with a tight jet-black pony tail dangling between her shoulder blades turns and dips her chin in a gesture of acknowledgement before she returns to smoking a cigarette out the window.

"I am just visiting. Pleased to meet you."

The man is wearing a full headset with headphones and typing gloves. As he greets you with a double trigger finger gesture he appears to have accidentally wiped away whatever he was coding or virtually manipulating. As he stacks items back in place you walk towards your bunk. The man sidesteps you, indicating he must have a real world overlay displayed across his virtual workspace.

"Yeah, visiting while you try and make a perfect three dimensional model of Cathy. Kick rocks, Grommet."

The embarrassed little man must be mean mugging his aggressor behind those goggles as he makes his exit.

"Call me Brubaker. I make wheels spin and things go boom. Cathy is an expert in logistics, and young Grommet there is one of the preeminent computer scientists in the country."

You amble to your bunk and notice the items on your desk: another papyrus card and a set of keys, one to open your trunk, one to open your desk, and one for an unknown vehicle. The papyrus has eight lines of self-explanatory information.

Dinner, Main Auditorium: Table Twenty-Three, 1830, Outfitting, Main Residence, 2100, Vehicle, License ZR81.

Two full hours until dinner, you decide against breaching Cathy's icy exterior, and have no interest in getting to know Brubaker. Flipping the keyring off the desk and forcefully catching it mid-air, the decision has been made to tour the grounds.

Leaving the barracks and walking behind the building you count six rooms down each side of your hallway, with three to a room this three story building can house one hundred and eight individuals. This section of the base has eight barracks, therefore half of the force at hand. Between these two particular barracks is a wide plot of cement serving as vehicle storage. A jaded few might have become accustomed to these lavish surprises around every corner, but your feet momentarily cease their shuffle as you are once again stopped in your tracks. Twelve Ford Broncos, ranging from 1969 to 1975, are lined perfectly in two rows of six, flashing reflections off waxed and rugged exteriors. Laughing to yourself you stand behind the one identifying itself as ZR81. This is an indigo 1975 Ford Bronco with a 302 V8 engine, Flowmaster exhaust, C-4 Transmission, Dana 20 transfer case, disc brakes, Rancho 9000 adjustable shocks, a 3.5 suspension lift, 33 inch BFGoodrich Mud Terrain Tires, dual gas tanks, and a Warn winch. Without feeling the need to kick the tires, you light the fires with the twist of the ignition. The vibrating chassis and throaty hum of the exhaust slaps a grin on your face, and once again you are thankful you know how to operate a manual transmission. Giddy up. You are touring your mysterious new home.

Looping around the barracks formation you carefully cut through a vineyard of unknown grape variety. The infinitely pleasing Mediterranean climate of California's central coast has baked the tilled soil until a sweet, humid musk lingers about you. This mixes with the unmistakable smell of that California ocean grown cannabis, as you spy a farmer wearing a traditional Asian conical hat, pantomiming a rolling of the dice with his right hand before he shoots it out as a fervent point in your direction, Zig Zag cigarette dangling from his lips. Bordering the vineyard is a patch of land that reminds you of the farm in Montecito, only this soil is producing voluminous strawberries, blueberries, and rows of green leafy vegetables. There is more white wooden fencing, and you tally cows, pigs, and strange chicken coop structures propped up on wooden wheels. Cracking rifles coax you into a cautious creep near a fifteen hundred yard outdoor shooting range. Black and brown fatigued men and women are prone, firing long range in semi-automatic rhythm, and beside them their compatriots are walking down paper targets with fully automatic fury, dropping the empty rifle as they advance, summersaulting behind cover, and unloading eleven opportunities for suffering with their secondary weapon.

Advancing into a more administrative section of the compound you peg a large cement building as the communications hub, mainly due to the array of satellite and radio equipment on the roof. Grommet, akin to a frazzled Tokyo businessman, scurries into a neighboring cement structure. This must house the computer lab. There is a tower that reminds you of the Venice Beach lifeguard headquarters, only three times as wide and three times as tall. Driving between those buildings you contemplate whether this is an observation deck for the base or a control tower for the airstrip stretching out into the mature grey California sagebrush. A lone Bombardier Challenger 350 stands polished and solemn under the vaulted metal of an open hangar.

Beyond the airstrip and nearing the foothills are slabs of cement covering enough square footage to make the average Los Angeles car dealership look like a McDonald's parking lot. There are seven columns of semi-trailer trucks boasting reflective, cylindrical double tankers. Eighteen wheel big rigs, columns running three deep, and you don't get the feeling these are filled with cow's milk. More perplexing is the seven column seven row formation of parked California Highway

Patrol cruisers. A lone cruiser is travelling at high speed on a vacant patch of cement with a large concrete divider running down the center. Suddenly the cruiser screeches into a skidding, oversteered drift, abruptly sticking to a ninety degree footprint of burnt rubber and smoke. The black and brown fatigued driver and two rear passengers leap from the vehicle, banging the magazines of their Beretta ARX 160 assault rifles on the hood and trunk of the vehicle, pointed somewhat in your direction. Things that make you go hmmm. Hastily removing yourself from that situation you find yourself driving past a crude concrete structure of four floors, sans walls or fourth floor ceiling. Perhaps a structure firemen would use to practice carrying equipment or work on tactical movement, only this structure is occupied by men guiding large steel wedges dangling from the hook of a construction crane. Guiding the wedges so that they hang two thirds on the concrete floor and one third off into space, they unhinge from the crane and use a winch system to pull the wedge flush with the floor. You watch them do this once, and then reattach the wedge to the crane. The crane dangles the wedge back to earth as the ground crew resets to begin the drill again. Finding yourself outside of barracks thirteen you have to ask directions back to the other formation of barracks buildings.

With the Bronco tethered behind your barracks you splash cold water on your face in the communal washroom. A measured pace returns you to the bunk. You remind yourself to maintain your integrity in this mad world, confident you possess complete control of your mind and body. The conversation in the rose garden replays in your head.

You never doubt your sanity. The truth is the truth, no matter how tempestuous the environment, you will always be a sum of your own actions. Time and tide wait for no one, groups of people are heading to the main auditorium.

6

The auditorium conjures classic images of humanity assembled, whether it be for politics, knowledge, treacherous plots, philosophical discourse, or safety in numbers. Grand in scale, a "foremost hall under heaven," this must be the atmosphere of King Hrothgar's great mead hall Heorot. Questions remain as to who amongst us will rise as Beowulf, ripping Grendel's limb from socket.

Table twenty-three is near the stage at the center of the auditorium. Each slab of cypress is designed like a picnic table with thirty settings of silver plates and cups. A bottle of wine produced at these very vineyards sits before each pair of settings. Most of the individuals are in the casual conversations of friends and acquaintances, only your table has that awkward silence brought on by the burden of the first move. Jeffrey is standing behind a control board on a stage that rises five feet off the ground. The ceiling rafters are outfitted with a range of spotlights, and there is a fifty by fifty foot screen behind the stage. Within a partially drawn curtain before the screen you make out the unmistakable shape of Mallory. She is clawing her fingernails playfully along the suited shoulder of a man with his back turned, silver hair longer than the traditional businessman. He is changing from a suit to the black and brown fatigues you know so well, but the darkness behind the curtains makes it difficult to determine much else. Mallory draws the curtain from her path and takes a seat near the control board. Jeffrey signals the number five with his hands and nods to someone offstage.

The wait staff has their own army, and they are deployed with all manner of beef, pork, rabbit, Brussel sprout, carrot, pear, spinach, and considering this is California, kale. You opt for a glass of Grenache and enjoy its smooth swirl on your palate as you await this event with great anticipation.

Jeffrey gets the nod and the lights dim until he unleashes the full force of the auditorium's ample sound system. Rage Against the Machine's *Take the Power Back* kicks in with the bass drum, the groaning guitar, and thumping slap bass. Jeffrey is dancing in place, jerking his knees up to near chest height, pointing out to the audience, then ripping his entire body into a whipping motion. As the lyrics kick in, a sixty-seven year old man with slicked back silver hair and a warm smile skips out onto the stage. With the roaring of the auditorium he works the crowd stage right to stage left. Nodding and pigeon walking, he is alternating between holding his hand to his ear for applause and pumping both upward facing palms from hip to head height. Skipping to the center of the stage he takes his mark, nodding his head, looks to Jeffrey, and in a throat slitting motion the music immediately stops.

"So nice to see all of you. Preaching. To. The Choir. Alright, so—"

A piercing voice cuts through the sound system like a hot knife through butter:

"Are you finally going to tell us what we've been doing out here the past three weeks, running around in circles and counting antelope?!"

"Well then! Who put a nickel in you, young lady? Wind it down. Wind, it, down."

Peter Triton is holding his hands to his brow like a visor, shielding the light so he can see who is speaking. As he identifies Catherine at one of the stage front tables he smiles and begins nodding his head slowly.

"Quite the specimen. I wonder who vetted you. Jeffrey?"

Triton is looking towards Jeffrey, then back to Catherine, then back to Jeffrey.

"I knew it was you, Jeffrey. I knew it was you."

Jeffrey is shaking his head, "She is one of the most distinguished in her company, boss. She spearheaded logistics on that airstrip in Djibouti."

"Of course. Of course. What do you think the purpose of this little speech is, young lady? Get this woman a Pinot Noir and some methaqualone."

The crowd is puzzled.

"My mistake, they don't make that anymore. Ok! Starting over. Should I come back out? Ok, here we go. All of you here today are confirmed patriots, sharing these times that try our souls. That, my friends, is a riff on Thomas Paine, but let me give you a direct quote. 'Those who expect to reap the blessings of freedom, must, like men, undergo the fatigues of supporting it.'"

The crowd almost unanimously smash their fists on the cypress tables, clanging their cutlery in recognition. Strutting the stage Triton puts his hand over the logo on his fatigues.

"When you wear this mark upon your breast you stand against tyranny, ignorance, and fanaticism. What is life when you pay ten times the worth of a muscular dystrophy drug for your child, just so a pharmaceutical company can meet shareholder demands? What is liberty when you have an adjustable rate mortgage and twenty-five percent interest credit card debt? How can you pursue happiness when our broken system can't protect us from violence, terror, tribal racism, or even crops that have pesticide spliced into the genome of the seed?!"

The clamor of fists on cypress, silver on silver, and fifteen hundred shouting humans fill the spacious interior. If only Grendel could hear us now.

"I will not apologize, folks, as I remind you we do not live in an absolute democracy. The United States is, always has been, and always will be a constitutional republic. Our founding fathers had more than a millennium worth of recorded history, they knew how the world was formed, how the world worked, and what the world could be. They did not squander this one single chance in this New World. In our great country officials are elected as representatives of the people, and they must govern according to the established constitutional law that clearly states the government's power over citizens. How do you think this is working out in 2020?!"

An eruption of roars precedes an aerial assault of pheasant and other fine, slow cooked meats.

"That is completely unnecessary! I applaud your enthusiasm, ladies and gentlemen, but what a waste of food, and now someone has to clean that up. Let us enjoy a few smooth snorts of these fine vintages and compose ourselves for a moment."

Triton walks over to the soundboard and takes a draw of water, a deep breath, composing himself, and licks the side of Mallory's face, surprising and embarrassing her before her eyes double in size while she smiles and adjusts her strategically partially unbuttoned fatigues.

"The system is broken, ladies and gentlemen. I think that is quite clear. Who should be a more staunch capitalist than yours truly, California's King Midas? Truth is, we became a socialist capitalist society when Roosevelt started rolling out the New Deal in 1933. Well, it's time for my new deal. We are going to reform our society so that it is once again based on the pursuit of our unalienable rights. There will be no sitting at the table if you bring nothing to it. If you can work, you will work. If you cannot, you will be cared for. If you can and you don't, you'll find life difficult and void of support. Look around you, you know what I call this farm? Yes, it may have a few pillboxes, an airstrip, self-sustained power grid, and a standing army, but it is a farm. I call it the Blueprint. Everything you are eating right now comes from our fields and flock. The cows graze on the grass and create the manure, the chickens eat the maggots out of the manure and fertilize the fields so there can be more grazing, and then they lay their eggs. As long as we respect nature we can hunt in these mountains, the harvest is bountiful. There is a natural ecosystem, a real circle of life we have completely lost touch with. We are being sold cancer. Multinational conglomerates have forced our farmers into indentured servitude, our citizens are slowly dying eating this Black Death, and all at the will of crony capitalism. Our system has failed us."

Muted, more somber fists on the table.

"We are going to press pause. Not forever, but for five years at least. We are going to return to feeding all of our citizens, to providing housing for all of our citizens, to providing crucial medicines and healthcare for the well-being of our citizens. This is the United States of America: the greatest civilization known to history, don't you think we can feed, house, and care for our people? It may be at the expense of GDP, but damn the bottom line. We are wiping out the status quo. For those that cannot hunt desert bighorn sheep and jackrabbits in their hills, we will provide them food, and they will provide us something in return. Forget this Calexit rubbish! By the way, who do you think consumes all of this

trash Hollywood is putting out these days? What would
Holmby Hills look like if everyone between Nevada and the
Carolinas stopped plunking down for that so called content?"

There is a palpable buzz of hope and admiration in the air.

"Technology is as much our foe as it is our ally. When we
make our move there won't exactly be an abundance of
capital for research and development, which is fine. Prepare
yourselves for a cultural Renaissance. Most of our
capabilities in regards to technology are earmarked for
medicine. Who knows better than I the power of technology?
Look at what I have accomplished. I can tell you we will treat
technology as a titanic cyclops that we will keep behind a
boulder in a cave, unleashing him on the rare occasions that
we harness him to further our mission. I reiterate, we are
only pressing pause. Imagine what this great nation can
accomplish once our citizens are cared for. Now this last part
might get a little scary for you, but take it from a man who
has studied economics extensively. Richard Nixon doomed
our country when he took the dollar off the gold standard.
Now, we are working out the specifics, but we are going to
base our currency on a combination of gold and Bitcoin held
in reserve by yours truly and this little gentlemen's club I'm
involved with. I've been stockpiling gold for over two
decades. We will base our currency on a gold standard in the
manner that Alexander Hamilton originally structured our
economy. This will protect us from corruption and tyranny.
Only thing is, this currency won't be called the dollar
anymore. See, the greenback was killed in 1971. The wealthy
can keep their property and possessions, but that bank

account won't be worth dirt. They can come and work with the rest of us."

The roar is deafening. Peter Triton ducks a silver plate thrown by a brave dissenter in the crowd.

"So with this new currency, backed by tangible wealth, we are going to create local credit unions that will loan money at extremely low, fixed interest rates so our economy can continue and homes can be purchased and mediocre films can be financed. There will be no international banks in this country. They're gone. They won't have much say in it either. Federal Reserve? With their power to control our economy and devalue our currency, these unelected bureaucrats steal money from the everyday American through their hidden tax of inflation. Never again will any amount of money be used to bail out a bank when it could be supporting a citizen. The Federal Reserve is unconstitutional and they have been terrorizing our nation for one hundred and seven years. Not anymore. Every one of you has been assigned a Bitcoin wallet, and each day you've been here you have received a wage, and each day you are here you will receive a wage. If you don't agree with this, you do not need to contribute, but I can't let you leave until we put this in motion."

The crowd laughs, some nervously. One person yells out from the back.

"What's this movement called?!"

"They'll give it a name, before we're done. You see, we do it, they talk about it. Now, in a short time I'm going to paint the broad strokes of how we're going to execute this mission. Following that, you will each be briefed in your respective companies by your company commanders. Catherine, I suppose that's you, I apologize. What we are going to do is take action, ring the bell so loud that it will be impossible to unring, and create enough leverage to force our agenda. These are not foregone conclusions, but rather the beginnings of a strongly worded dialogue. They can get in line or get out of the way. Now in closing, this entire endeavor depends on the three S's. Surprise. Speed. Security. You will continue to have no communication outside of this farm. I know the computer guys can probably find a way, but is it worth eating a bullet? Any communication requests will be run through Mallory's team, she is running comms. So, ladies and gentlemen, enjoy your meal and train hard. Now, some of you have earned your emblems."

Triton motions to a few people who bring large plastic bags full of cloth badges. He jumps from the stage and walks to the head of the table where Brubaker is seated. Taking the first bag of embroidered patches in his hands he beams with a smile, and before he tosses it in the air towards his faithful:

"Hundred-Handers!"

Everyone cheers as he tosses the company their badges. Walking to the next table.

"Highway Cerberus!"

"Tower Overlords!"

"Silent Darkness!"

"Winged Sentinels!"

"Everything is on the table! There are no limits! Enjoy your chocolate con churros. I look forward to working with you."

With that he takes Mallory by the hand and begins his exit. You are blown away while you enjoy the finest meat you've tasted, the freshest vegetables to crunch between your teeth. The wait staff serve dessert: porcelain cups of melted chocolate, plates of churros, and coffee. You recall an appointment for "outfitting" in forty-five minutes and spend the time chatting with a table that seems mostly enthused, partially concerned.

The main residence is appropriately the most exquisite work of colonial architecture on the base. The building is a house in five sections with a five-bay two story central block, surrounded by two story end wings which connect to the central block via a one story hyphen on either side. The central bay door frame is engaged with Ionic columns, and the second floor windows are framed by an entablature.

A servant is standing before the exterior shrubbery and nods as you approach. His uniform is identical to the servants in Montecito, only this man is plump, rosy cheeked and jovial.

"Your punctuality is appreciated! Master awaits in the ballroom. This way, please."

Sauntering through the main entrance, and climbing the stairs to a spacious ballroom, you stand patiently as the perplexed servant opens his mouth and raises his finger in anticipation four times, turning towards empty space in succession.

"Down here, Peckwith! I told you to direct our guest to the drawing room!"

The servant straightens his posture, and without missing a beat leads you back downstairs and into a drawing room, directing you to another green suede chair while he stands beside the door with his head bowed. Peter Triton capers down the hall and into the room.

"You haven't been taking your medication, Peckwith. Why do I go to the trouble of retaining that pretty young thing to separate your doses if you're just going to spit a green Louie into my eye whenever we have company? About your business, old friend, about your business."

"Very good, sir."

As Peckwith takes his leave Peter shakes your hand with gusto and circumvents the linen draped desk at the center of the room.

"Peter. A pleasure. If only you had met dear Peckwith in the '90s, never have you heard a soul recite Kipling with such passion. Now pick your poison."

Pulling the linen with the zest of a magician, Triton gestures towards the desk with the open palms and plastic smile of a gameshow model showcasing prizes. There is a Steyr AUG assault rifle, a SIG SG 516, an S&T Daewoo K11, a BAE Systems L85, and a magazine of .50 BMG cartridges.

"First of all, sir, I must tell you how much I appreciate your hospitality and the opportunity to make a large scale impact. You're talking to the wrong person if you're looking for someone to shoulder a rifle and fire downrange on our countrymen. I have a weapon, which I brought with me, and I will use it to defend my life and only in that fashion."

"Yes, we took a peek into your personal carry-on during the Montecito visit. Quite a nifty little blade in your possession, I might add. I'm sure Mallory slept a mite bit sounder with the additional armament on premises. As I reach for a peach. Speaking of which, my yacht was leading through the second day of regattas during a recent Gaglia Rolex Cup, the portion in the Bay of Saint-Tropez. I was with my second wife: erotic novelist Emily Dubois, wildly popular. After a five star dinner at Le Girelier I had to go kick down a few doors to get someone to open the Hermès boutique. This maillons déchaînés reversible silk and cashmere scarf was just screaming at me through the window. Took about an hour to find the shopkeep, and about fifteen minutes more for Jeffrey to alert me that wifey was being a little too popular, and a little too erotic, back at Hôtel de Paris. Short story long, she doesn't write erotic novels anymore, or do much of anything for that matter, and if that young man is still waiting tables I can assure you it is with great difficulty. We decided it would be in the best interest of both our crew and the French government to forfeit the remaining three days of the race. I sailed to Genoa that night, hopped on the Bombardier, executed a wire transfer somewhere over the Atlantic, and didn't have to field so much as a single inquiry after the wheels hit the tarmac."

You stand in silence, confused and disgusted at the dichotomy of this man.

"Perspective is all that is. I had a feeling you would decline the rifle. The human mind is the greatest weapon on this planet. Some people, you could drop them naked in the forest and the grizzlies would be in trouble. I have an important job for you, you'll be working closely with Jeffrey. Here is your emblem, some specialized fatigues, and this."

Triton reaches into a drawer and tosses you an Alaskan chest holster fitted to your Smith and Wesson. Black leather straps sling over one shoulder and cross your ribs to comfortably and securely holster the revolver against your chest. The fatigues are still black and brown, only the Triton logo is blacked out and your fatigues are covered in webbing. He has also provided a lightweight rig with belt and hip pockets.

"I'm not going to kill anybody."

"If this goes according to plan, no one has to die. Training starts tomorrow, and you're going to get thirteen weeks' worth of Oohrah squeezed into a very tight timetable. Sleep well."

Peckwith arrives to escort you out, and upon your exit you overhear him:

"Sir, there is a group outside wishing to dissent."

"Treat them with respect. I'll talk to them. Get Guthrie on the horn."

Carrying your gear back to barracks you are examining the emblem. The embroidered image is a ninja in full black camouflage hanging ten on the nose of a soaring C-130, the military's omnipresent four engine turboprop transport aircraft. CLOUD PROWLERS is embroidered in large black lettering below this image. Brubaker is snoring and secreting alcohol fumes. Catherine's bunk is empty. You drift off to sleep curious what tomorrow will hold.

Your dream envisages a torrent of water flowing from the center of a jagged mountain. Perched atop is an enormous creature, part man and part beast, from its arms curl the heads of dragons, and from its thighs massive coils of vipers extend up to his head and emit a menacing hiss. The creature reaches down and breaks off a jagged slab of stone and gashes its own throat with a ferocious rip.

As the head falls back you see within the spreading neck wound an indigo sky with black clouds, dark waves crashing against charcoal cliffs to the steady, muffled roar of the ocean.

7

Corrosion of Conformity's *Long Whip/Big America* slowly increases in volume as you navigate artichoke tinted brush leading into the laurel green hills of a dew swept, hazy dawn arena. Following music that piercingly contrasts this serene environment you arrive at a flat portion of this mountainous terrain, per Jeffrey's instructions. The man himself is sitting on a plastic crate smoking a Winston, surveying the turquoise creek at the base of the next ridge. Beside him are two muscled recruits, Hundred-Handers. He presses a switch on his boombox.

"Rook, today you have been promoted to Private. I take this process very seriously, and so will you. Do not speak unless spoken to and do not question these methods. Your job is to show up, shut up, and work hard. Meet Tweedledee and Tweedledum."

The recruits are not twins. Both silently imposing, one is black and the other is of Japanese descent.

"Hand to hand."

As dawn tiptoes into morning you spend the next few hours slowly and silently advancing on a succession of three men. With your hands raised chin level you advance on Tweedledee, dispossessing him of a wooden crutch symbolizing a rifle, stabbing him with the phantom bayonet. You advance to Tweedledum, disarming him of his chopped foam bat symbolizing a machete, wrenching his wrist and spinning his body as you slit his throat and throw him aside. You produce a plastic knife from your rig and advance on Jeffrey, thrusting the knife to his throat and sidestepping to your right to stab him in the lungs. You reset, walking back to the top of the line, and do this again, and again, and again. Sometimes two of you duel with the wooden rifles, the goal is to bayonet them before they bayonet you. Sometimes you advance exclusively with the foam bat: cutting jugular, slicing stomach, thrusting liver, advancing to the next man. The only sound is the smothering of chaparral, the crunching of California fescue under your boot, their inflorescence hitchhiking along your pant legs. Water break with the morning sun, followed by a seven mile run. You return to base and eat like royalty. Catherine's bunk is empty. Brubaker yammers incessantly. You are too tired for nightmares.

Today you are in an Olympic sized swimming pool, strapped to a chair surrounded by piping. Jeffrey stands in front explaining this is practice for helicopter evac. Tweedledee and Tweedledum grasp the piping and flip your chair upside down underwater, you release all the buckles and straps and swim to the surface. Repeat ad nauseam. Ten mile run. Ratatouille, smoothest crème brûlé on record. No nightmares.

This time Tweedledee and Tweedledum wait for you to swim towards their position, then put you in an underwater headlock until you fight your way to freedom. You swim two hundred fifty yards in the pool with a fifty pound pack. Back to headlocks. Another swim. Tweedledee tells you he was a mechanical engineering student at the University of California, Irvine. His name is Joshua. Jeffrey tells him to shut up and throws an empty pack of cigarettes in your face. You forego wine at dinner.

Marching to the creek in the mountains Tweedledum tells you he was Joshua's roommate at U.C. Irvine. His name is Shiro. Civil engineering. Jeffrey has strung barbed wire across the creek for two hundred yards. You spend the day crawling on your back, half submerged, while he sprays automatic gunfire into the earth and rock above your face. Fifteen mile hump with a fifty pound pack. You sleep like a baby.

Jeffrey has led you much farther into the forest than any previous excursion. Visibility is excellent, the occasional bishop pine and a sea of incense cedar shelter the spines of seemingly limitless mountains. Fifty pound packs on your backs, he hands you a map and begins instructing the basics of navigation. He teaches you the compass, how to find water in valleys or how to collect dew with your sock, how to build a fire against a rock so it will reflect heat. He shows you how to make a stretcher by tying your fatigues across two branches. You silently eat MREs perched on a ridge, breathing oxygen rich air void of car exhaust, fast food aroma, and the scent of bus stop urine.

"You know, his real name is Simon."

"What? Why does he go by Peter?"

"You'd have to ask him that. After my stretch of time on his team I don't think it's natural for one man to have more money than ten generations could spend. He preaches equality, but sometimes it's obvious he wants to be worshipped. The ego in all of us."

You march back in tandem, silent. Would it be different if it was you that had these means? Could you lead these people? For every blessing we have a curse. Dinosaurs roamed the earth for two hundred million years. We have existed for two hundred thousand; civilization as we know it is struggling after six thousand years of existence. What does that say about the human race? Are we meant to be here, will the earth cast us into nothing like a dog shaking off fleas? You feel our goodness is innate, but too much power is in the grasp of darkness. Why was it you in the rose garden? Do you believe?

The next day is low-key. Jeffrey informs you there will be night op training in a few hours. He shows you how to twist up grass and foliage and slip it into the webbing of your fatigues to create an improvised ghillie suit.

"Go hit chow. Drag this suit behind your Bronco while you cruise around base. Helipads at 2100."

Lunch is coq au vin. Resting in your bunk there is too much eager anticipation to drift wholly unconscious. From the unseen black chamber beyond the horizon rises a new moon, this razor thin crescent.

Jeffrey is standing at the door to the AugustaWestland AW101 with no armaments. He is wearing standard black and brown Triton fatigues, holding a black duffel bag. Gesturing for you to come aboard, he points to the pilot. A jet turbine kicks to life, yet the rotors remain motionless despite this sonic crescendo. The interior is preposterously luxurious and unexpected considering the military styling of the exterior. You sit in the front compartment on one of two white leather captain's chairs facing each other, divided by a wood finished tabletop. Jeffrey takes his seat across from you.

"I've been briefed on our battalion's first operation. I'm being polite when I say battalion, because in reality this critical set-up for our overarching endeavor, well it is a two person op. One of those people is me."

Out the window you can see the shadow of the blades in the observation tower spotlight. The jet blare is peaking as the rotors begin to move. Jeffrey produces two Heinekens from his duffel bag. Gyrating his wrist in front of his face he uses the flesh of his bare forearm to twist and pop the bottle caps.

"I am promoting you to Private First Class. You are about to take your final exam. Make it through this and the second person on the op is you. Let's go through some hand signals."

Jeffrey puts his thumb to his lips and raises his pinkie in a chug-a-lug motion, handing you the Heineken.

"Seriously though, I'm going to expect you to signal these back to me from memory later. Pay attention."

The rotors are at full speed as you feel your stomach drop slightly when the aircraft leaves the ground with significant lift.

"A clear concise 'I' shape with your arm means you have information. When I put my fist to my chest that means I have an order. Flexed, arched fingers in the shape of a question mark means you have a question."

The thin crescent moon barely illuminates the Ponderosa pine and California black oak as you bank and tilt above mountains. Jeffrey puts his finger to his lips.

"Shhh. Self-explanatory. Touch your pointer finger to your thumb and extend the other three fingers, that's 'Ok chief, I hear you.' Hand over your brow like a visor is telling me to look at something."

The jet engine portion of the aircraft has calmed, the chopping rotors sound akin to a traditional helicopter, though this is significantly muted in comparison to the ghetto birds back home. The spotlights back at base are out of view.

"Cup my hand to my ear, I want you to listen. Hand to the throat refers to a hostage. If I do a windshield wiper motion that means disregard. If I pat my head, I want you to cover me. If I pat my head and point at you, I'll be covering you. Alright, your promotion comes with some new kicks."

Jeffrey reaches into his duffel bag and hands you a pair of HAIX Ranger GSG9 S Tactical Boots.

"Gofasters. Here's a polyester layer for under your ghillie suit, and some gloves, I know you're a Californian. Don't worry, I won't peek."

Jeffrey cracks another Heineken. You deduce by the pace of his drinking and the casual set of fatigues he won't be joining you. G-force presses your body into the white leather. With the banking cabin, ocean is now visible from the window to your right. The aircraft begins to hover and slowly decrease in altitude. Jeffrey heads to the back of the cabin while you add layers under your fatigues. You hear the humming zip of rope drawn through a carabiner.

"Walk heel toe out there, and keep a low profile. Can you imagine the honeymooners at Big Sur River Inn getting an eyeful of this crazy getup? Methinks a police presence would materialize in short order. People are liable to mistake you for some kind of 2020 Zodiac."

Jeffrey attaches a carabiner to your rig and another to an anchor on the cabin floor. Sliding open the door he takes a deep breath.

"Eat the pressure, taste the pain. Make it back to the base and you've got the job. Don't fall."

Jeffrey stuffs two maps in your pack and gives you the hand signal for, "Well, we're waiting."

Without receiving any previous instruction in rappelling you gather your courage, grip the rope with your left hand, and step off the edge of the hovering helicopter. Ever so slightly letting the rope feed through with your right brake hand, you awkwardly and gradually approach the ground, realizing it was probably no more than a fifteen foot drop. Unhooking the carabiner you look upwards to catch Jeffrey's third Heineken cap with your face. Cackling like an evil villain from Hollywood's gilded age, he collects the rope as the helicopter thrusts skyward and across the Douglas-fir and coastal redwood. Shortly thereafter you find yourself in complete darkness save a sliver of moon, the din of a shadowy coast, and the shrill songs of crickets.

Click. Studying the map, you need a landmark. Click. Crunching in the darkness you creep towards the detached sound of traffic toning with an enthusiastic shore. The shrubbed hill you are kneeling on is above the immediate tree line, and you laugh when you realize Jeffrey was not being facetious with his warning of tourist interaction. Behold this Chevron station beside a highway. The buzzing artificial brightness of the metal-halide bulbs feel inappropriate in this natural setting. Closer inspection yields the Big Sur Library and two collections of cabins, the Ripplewood Resort and Glen Oaks. A powerfully wheezing elderly man ambles four feet in front of you as you observe this location undetected. The highway is California State Route 1, named Cabrillo

Highway at this stretch. Back on the shrubbed hill and behind the cover of a few trees you click back your flashlight and examine the map. You are two miles east of Pfeiffer Beach. The hump back to base is approximately fifteen to twenty miles, as the crow flies. With a full stomach and water in your pack you determine this is conceivable as long as you maintain your wits and balance; a tumble off these ridges would return you to nature indefinitely. You have all night, take it slow and steady. The Ventana Double Cone towers defiantly along your most direct route. You would prefer to avoid this prominent twin mountain top with an elevation of nearly five thousand feet. Perhaps you can circumvent, but you have come to terms with the fact that the path home will consist entirely of mountainous terrain. Plodding down the hill you link up with Juan Hiquera Creek, deciding the most attractive strategy is following the various creeks and rivers along the valleys, avoiding an arduous elevation climb when possible. The streams and tributaries will provide manageable hiking along their riverbeds, and more importantly serve as crucial markers to aid in your navigation.

The fear of the unknown wanes now that your plan is formulated and under execution. "Ain't nothin' to it, but to do it." Where did you hear that? You realize this time spent alone is a blessing. Every sound is amplified, if a twig broke a mile in any direction you would know. There is a cold moisture in the air as if the night was flirting with rain. The temperature is in the low forties, quite manageable and almost pleasant considering your layering and physical exertion. The creek babbles as boughs squeak and groan in the wind, leaves softly rattling. Why did it take such an extreme set of events to push you into this magnificent scenery? This was always accessible while you had a car. Always forgotten. Taking a draw off your hydration pack you continue walking and scarf down an MRE nut and raisin mix. As the creek ends you climb a steep slab of dirt caked mountain, some secluded pariah of a crag singled out by an arid microclimate. The subsequent crossing of a man-made trail determines you are navigating effectively. You reach Doolans Hole Creek and a forest of black walnut. Your course is plotted northeast as you break from the creek, this portion will be difficult up and over umber mountains to Ventana Mesa Creek. The twinkling glances of the stars appear warm and embracing. The voice of Ralph Waldo Emerson reminds "nature never wears a mean appearance." Your mind travels to the recent past and you wholeheartedly disagree, but you get where he was coming from. You also remember, "Motion or change, and identity or rest, are the first and second secrets of nature: Motion and Rest."

You begin encountering piles of white, decaying scat as you continue trudging along what is either a deer trail or a path carved by the footsteps of Esselen Native Americans. Possibly bear scat—the northwestern black bear populates the Klamath Forest portion of the state, the California black bear dances the forests from Santa Cruz to San Diego— however, the feces pile is too small for a bear, and the pile is too large for a deer. You find it interesting the piles seem strategically placed on a path, when essentially the entire world can serve as an animal's toilet. Drawing on your hydration pack you stop for a moment to devour two MRE marble cakes. It has been rough going, but you don't want to stop for too long knowing you may succumb to prolonged repose.

Pride beams from within once you stand on the ridge overlooking Ventana Mesa Creek, listening to the rush of the small waterfall and breathing the aggressively oxygenated atmosphere courtesy of the sycamore. According to your map the Ventana Mesa Creek intersects with the Carmel River in Hiding Canyon, your halfway marker. Walking along the ridge you make the conscious effort to watch your footing, knowing a foolish step is the primary danger, until you notice another pile of scat, not white but richly chestnut. Mountain lion. What other animal could make a pile that size? Drawing water and chewing another steady supply of salty carbohydrates you perk your ears. Nothing but the balanced rush of the creek below. You shine your powerful light along the ridge and riverbed: only greenery. "Art and luxury work as enhancement and sequel to this original beauty."

Navigating along Carmel River you approach intersecting waterways at what is either Blue Creek or Bear Basin Creek. Either way, you are planning to continue east along Carmel River into Pine Valley. Flashlight beaming and attached to your rig, you stop in your tracks. Another pile of scat, chestnut brown with a hint of Reseda green, wafting steam like a miniature Manhattan manhole. Fresh. You touch the butt of the seven shot .357 Magnum revolver strapped to your chest. This is clearly marked territory.

Your mind races. One third of your hydration pack remains filled as you take a few quick draws and stomach an MRE apple turnover. You're out here with a two hundred pound ambush predator that can run forty or fifty miles per hour. The fear returns, jolting your nervous system. You imagine walking down a rocky path before crumbling into a few hundred pounds of thrashing sinew, fur, cloth, and equipment. Powerful jaws piercing the base of your skull and snapping your spine. If you had the chance to hear the beast, or put eyes on it, it would only require one hollow point to deliver a potentially mortal wound. Still, you would need to make shots count considering your skull would be crushed like a watermelon on sidewalk before the cougar bled out.

Traversing the range, listening to the rustle of leaves stemming from branches on ancient trees, the harmony of nature supports your fragile psyche. Fear is the wrong mindset. This emotion is replaced with what is most accurately described as respect. You are the stranger in this animal's territory, and though the hierarchy is being established, you are sharing this landscape. Walking softly, deliberately, quietly, your mind begins to ease. You have never been so alert, so alive, so in tune with reality. In the earth's truest form you have found your highest plane of awareness. You don't need this gun, and you wouldn't use it if you encountered the natural embodiment of this raw energy you cannot see, but know is there, not far off, observing.

Carmel River trails off into the aptly named Pine Valley. You link up with another Esselen footpath and admit to yourself that you are exhausted. Who said this had to be completed by sunrise? You feel at peace, in the zone, and not against bunking amongst a thousand acres and one mountain lion versus a few hundred square feet and one flatulent Brubaker. A shallow cave appears scooped into the mountain towards the end of this path. You gather sticks and kindling, using your lighter to easily make a fire. Adding more wood the fire is soon quite large, and you are pleased with your timing as the watch beeps 0400.

Deciding a tarantula check is necessary for your mental state you examine the cave. An abundance of white lines painted on the rock wall form a multitude of hands. There is no way to determine who painted these rocks, but the faded color and seemingly ancient style suggests Native Americans made these marks hundreds or even thousands of years ago. You press your palm against a painting that perfectly mirrors your own hand. The chilled stone, the authentic humanity, what intense connection you are experiencing.

"We are man, not beast. We have hands. We are family. We love."

You use your pack as a pillow and recline by the fire, allowing the heat to reflect off the cave wall. In this witching hour there is only the crackle of the snapping fire. Not even a breeze. You are drifting off.

Grrraaaaaooooooooooooooohhhwwwwww.

Eyes wide. More adrenaline than fear. Appreciation. You feel the connection. You are honored.

There is no longer any hope for sleep, you have to respect the situation, but you rest there for a few hours and let your body recuperate. A few sweeps of your flashlight in the off chance you can catch an iridescent ocular reflection, but your suspicions of the animal's proficiencies prove true. You slowly chew on an MRE BBQ beef sandwich. Sipping only enough water to wash it down. Dawn's dim light washes over the terrain.

Eyeballing an empty fire watchtower at Chews Ridge you confirm your position. You are at five thousand eighty-two feet elevation. Walking along this ridge you encounter another pile of scat, this time shaded black. This is the home stretch as the time is approaching 0900 with only a few miles left.

Descending the foothills leading into the base you easily spot Jeffrey stroking his chin during a conversation with a young woman in fatigues. She looks in your direction, and he turns to see you before his face lights up with joy and relief.

"Congratulations, Lance Corporal! After lunch we were going to muster a search party."

You approach Jeffrey, clap his palm, and pull him into a thankful embrace, before silently walking past him towards barracks.

Portland based Holman Air-Crane doesn't generally field much business during this half of December. Mr. Holman would rather be listening to the clinking of ice against a Collins glass down at the Horse Brass Pub.

"Estrada! Two sky cranes. Montgomery and Washington. Clay and Sansome. Need 'em built in a week."

"Yeah, let me get right on that."

"I'm serious, Estrada. If you're planning on being at Christmas dinner I suggest you get to work. Keep it efficient, but pay whatever rates get them built in time. This is non-negotiable. VIP grade clientele. Besides, I need the money, and I'm still calculating your bonus. Capisce?"

Officer Guillermo Morales has been dating Gia for two months now. He had a feeling she liked him, and despite having no strategy for asking out the barkeep, he frequented her work until the opportunity presented itself. Now they were going to spend New Year's Eve in Las Vegas, a real test for their budding relationship. Officer Morales is walking on sunshine straight into the King City Police Department headquarters.

"Chief, I'd like to take four days for New Year's."

"That's impossible, Morales."

"Chief, I've only used two days all year! Gia—"

"Can that, Morales. This is above my pay grade, and way above yours. No one is getting New Year's off."

You slept ten hours after that hump from Pfeiffer Beach. Your internal clock is out of whack, but according to Jeffrey this will be to your benefit. You are living up to the prowler half of your company handle. Wide awake at 2200 and walking the base you happen upon an impromptu hoops tourney. Jeffrey keeps calling you Sierra Hotel when you find him under the hole, as he effortlessly doles out uncalled offensive fouls and scores the gimme buckets. Shiro has rapid reflexes and a strange dependence on bank shots. Joshua plays excellent defense but can't shoot worth a lick, explaining he was an Army brat, spending most of his high school days playing central defender for football squads across Europe. Brubaker clarifies the only sport where he's from involves ducks and twenty gauge shotguns. Grommet passes the ball at every possession and steps out of the way in the lane.

Jeffrey tells you to get rest, eat a late breakfast, get more rest, and report to the main residence. Legitimate op is going down tomorrow night.

"Volume is about to get turned way up."

161

8

Upon your arrival Peckwith is nowhere in sight. You're on time and decide to let yourself in. Following the sound of a muttered voice emanating from just beyond one of the hyphen corridors, you happen upon the princess of pulchritude herself, leaning over a desk and practically spilling out of her fatigues. Mallory is on the satellite phone:

"Quite sure of it, less than two weeks. Just need confirmation on a few variables."

Her eyes rise from the desk to the doorway, with a heated expression and her hand over her chest she marches to the door and closes it in your face. Returning to the central block you discover Peckwith shadowboxing in unintentional slow-motion while facing Jeffrey.

"Save me from Henry Cooper."

Peckwith leads you to a converted bedroom towards the rear of the building. After fifteen minutes Mallory enters the room carrying a large camera case. Placing it before you:

"This is a Lensicon Optik 12k 7x42 Laser Rangefinder Binocular. Waterproof, GPS, photo and video capabilities, night vision, five mile range. These are durable, but be careful, we only have three and they cost more than a new Honda Civic."

Activating the front wall she pulls up an image of California, drawing an x on our location.

"Simplicity is the key to executing a plan. 2200, you will be transported from here, to here."

She has drawn another x in the Santa Lucia mountain range twenty-five miles to the southeast and connects the two with a line. Drawing another line while speaking:

"You will hike here to United States Army Reserve command post Fort Bowman and conduct reconnaissance until 1000. Extraction will be at the point of insertion. Document everything. Vehicles, personnel, movement patterns, possible entry points, building functions, and armament. Use the Lensicon, it will provide exact measurements via imagery, but I want you to make notes as well."

Jeffrey stands and pulls you up by the collar of your fatigues.

"They'll never know we're there."

At the helipad you are in full ghillie suit. The revolver is strapped to your chest, the rig contains food and water, you are wearing a diaper, and you have two notebooks and four golf pencils. Jeffrey arrives in a ghillie suit and black face paint. A Heckler & Koch MP5 is slung over his shoulder, resting on his stomach. In his arms is a Barrett M107A1 .50 caliber sniper rifle, boasting a Leupold Mark 4 ER/T 34mm scope. The jet turbine of the AugustaWestland shrieks as you mount up and depart.

"You have all the tools for this mission. If we are discovered, this bad boy will disable any vehicle pursuing us. Let's not cross that bridge, ok? There could be a few hundred soldiers, or a few thousand, depending on their training cycle and the reality of our depleted budgets."

Strange how completing a task one time can ease the anxiety of subsequent attempts. Despite the sands of the hour glass slipping towards a scenario placing you on the possible business end of a few hundred rifles, there is not much fear of the unknown swimming around your stomach.

The gale force of the rotors press parched shrubbery and crabgrass against the dusty floor. Kneeling in the dirt you half-smile at the now familiar image of a noisy aircraft abandoning you in nature, while the calm cool air between the oaks patiently surrounds you and Jeffrey.

"Stay low and slow. We are going to circle the base counter clockwise from the southwest. When we get to the two o'clock position I'm going to set the bipod and provide overwatch while you finish documenting the perimeter. Only hand signals. Snap the Lensicon and document in the notebook. Take your time, we're going to be there long enough for you to use that diaper more than once. Every few minutes look in my direction to see if I have anything that needs communicating. If that can't wait and you're in range I'll use this clicker here. If you're too far away I might hit you with a ruffed grouse, maybe a hooded merganser, a California quail, I'm sick with the bird calls."

Laughter. You are laughing out loud walking towards a military base. Crazy world.

"Don't lose focus and don't get careless. These soldiers deserve respect, don't forget they have a job to do and will not hesitate to turn out your lights. Our greatest advantage is that we are on American soil and they don't know we exist. Don't expect them to be in a constant state of alert, but stay frosty."

You arrive at a paved road twisting through the topography. This must be a main artery for the troops when they head into the mountains for training. Compared to the other night this is easy work. After a few miles the road descends sharply and cuts between two foothills, opening into a deep valley nestled in the mountains. The military base covers the entirety of this valley, though to your surprise this base has a significantly smaller footprint compared to Triton's compound. You take your position in the foothills to the west of the base and press the rubber cups of the Lensicon below your brow.

Brilliant green light seeps into your brain, everything is so clear. You cycle between night vision, some manner of black and white enhanced overlay, zero amplification, and back to night vision. The display reticle is spitting out data for distance, height, and whatever the letter I stands for. A Jeep on slow patrol catches your eye on a cursory sweep of the western perimeter, the Lensicon is displaying speed measurements for this object. Zooming out for a panoramic view you decide to focus on the outside and move inwards. Two thousand five hundred fifteen feet in front of you is a small building with a tile roof. There are solar panels to the right of the building. Zooming further, you sit and watch this building for a few moments until you spot movement of a uniformed soldier inside. Guard shack. Snap. GPS location and image captured. Three hundred feet from the guard shack is the western perimeter fence, which is also not as tall or as well guarded as the Triton fencing. Scanning behind the fence there are six H shaped concrete areas beside a one runway airstrip. Eight of the twenty-four possible corners of H are occupied by AH-64 Apache attack helicopters. On a large spread of concrete to the right of the airstrip are three immense transport aircraft that you recognize from your emblem as Lockheed C-130 Hercules. Snap.

There is nothing but grassland in front of the guard shack. Jeffrey motions for you to follow him along the base of the foothills until you are south of the base amongst a grove of maple trees. At this elevation it is difficult to see over the fencing. You scan and zoom, there are three reservoirs, two are full of water and one seems drained and slimed over. From this position you are looking straight on at the main entrance. Two small buildings for the guards, there are six guards at the main entrance. They seem relaxed. Snap. Crickets croon while you pause to take a deep breath of clean air. Civilization's only sound is the Jeep motor to the northwest, choking and grunting as gears spin and idle. Something is rustling in the maples, a chipmunk or bird, twigs and dust fall softly on a bed of fiery orange leaves. You shift your position with the loud crunching of dying foliage. Jeffrey's black face becomes one third exaggerated sclera when he signs the "quiet" hand signal. Jeffrey signals to continue away from the main entrance and towards the southeast portion of the base.

One kilometer south of the main entrance you crawl on your stomach across the road and into a thick collection of oak trees. Gaining elevation, you settle in another collection of oaks at a three-way intersection of small roads outside of the eastern perimeter fencing. There are a dozen or so buildings between the airstrip and the eastern fencing of this southern portion of the base. A substantial blacktop lot is chock-full of Humvees, eight wheeled IAV Stryker armored fighting vehicles, tank treaded Bradley armored fighting vehicles, Medium Tactical Vehicle Replacement cargo trucks, M35 two and a half ton cargo trucks, forklifts, and shipping containers. Far too many to count, let logistics sort that out. Snap. Jeffrey signals "wait one hour" at this location to rest, hydrate, and determine the function of the buildings. The golf pencil makes a few marks in your notebook. Maple pork sausage patty, maple muffin top MRE.

The dozen buildings are in the Spanish style with white walls and a terracotta tile roof, and more importantly, appear unoccupied. There may be a few hundred soldiers on this base, but there are certainly not a few thousand, at least at this moment. This is a reserve base, and a training base, so it seems logical that there would not be a full rotation of troops spending Christmas learning how to spit Hellfire missiles from Apaches and race Bradley fighting vehicles down the mountainsides.

Travelling northwest along the eastern fencing you spot four columns of buildings, nine buildings deep, with rooftop solar panels. Barracks. Lights out, dead quiet. Laughter draws your attention up the hill to your right. Jeffrey performs the visor signal, points to you, points to his chest, and points to the hills. Crawling on your stomach you reach six scattered white buildings outside of the main fencing. There is a parking lot with approximately thirty spaces, all empty. Three of the buildings appear full of whooping and hollering soldiers. You creep in for a closer look like a teenager roaming a residential neighborhood past curfew, peeking in kitchen windows. Surprised at your cavalier attitude you remind yourself this is not a game, you are not bulletproof, check yourself. Soldiers, presumably off duty, are shouting over video games, playing cards, listening to music, philosophizing, and reading. You count about a dozen in each of the first two buildings. Auxiliary barracks. For a complete survey you decide to risk it and crawl between these two buildings to get a look at the third. Sheltered amid tall grass and two beautiful Oregon ash trees you are about to take a knee and peer into the third building when you hear someone strangling a wild turkey. Pressing your body into the grass you quickly realize this is what passes for Jeffrey's bird call. Seconds later you hear footsteps on gravel. Without looking up you can feel the presence of someone leaning against one of the ash trees. The sound of scraping flint and the slow inhalations of a smoker enjoying every drag. You're unable to determine if your position is compromised. Blind faith. Jeffrey told you he was done killing, you're not counting on him turning this person into a soup sandwich with the .50 cal. Maybe a distraction, maybe he would choose you over his promises. You close your eyes and control your breathing, angry at your foolish maneuvers. For all your bold claims about heeding that inner voice you are a victim of pushing the envelope, taking that one extra step when your better judgement told you not to. The grind of a boot twisting into gravel. Moments later footsteps dissipate in the direction of the third building. You identify three men in the final building, two sleeping and one reading, before you join Jeffrey in the hills east of the base. Jeffrey puts his hand to his throat, and you can't tell if he's saying you're choking this mission, or if you should have taken that soldier hostage.

You have completed reconnaissance on the entire southern half of a base that is two miles from nose to toes. Complete silence during the slow ascension of the mountains one mile to the east of the thirty-six main barracks structures. Jeffrey extends the titanium bipod on the M107A1 and begins covering the rifle with foliage similar to what is inserted into the webbing of his ghillie suit. You are prone beside him, Lensicon pressed to your eye sockets. The northern half of the base has significantly more occupied parking spaces that border possible administration buildings. Snap. Five X shaped structures form a wedge with a U shaped structure in the center. Zooming for movement you snap pictures of several non-uniform individuals. Perhaps a hotel of some sort. Unexpected. Scanning five hundred feet northeast of the presumed hotel structures you focus on a wide rectangular building. No movement or lights at these wee hours of the morning, but you decide to watch for ten minutes while you enjoy two MRE cinnamon buns and discreetly use your diaper. Glancing over at Jeffrey, his right eye is locked into the scope, he did not notice. Focusing back on the dark building you zoom tight on a vehicle: USPS emblem. Post office, hotel, minimum guard detail, world class weaponry. Another large slab of blacktop is dotted with cargo trucks. As you scan and zoom the hairs stand up on the back of your neck. You're counting them out, nineteen in a row and four off to the side.

"Abrams," whispers Jeffrey, picking up on your silent excitement. The only word he has spoken in four hours.

Twenty-three M1 Abrams third generation battle tanks, each with sixty-eight tons of depleted uranium mesh-reinforced composite armor and forty rounds of 120 mm shells, not to mention nine hundred rounds of .50 caliber heavy machine gun for backup. Snap.

It is clear most of the fencing and barriers are to the south where highways converge with the main road into the base. The small road from the north is surrounded by mountainous terrain. Still, you note this is a paved road. You want to get a closer look at the northern portion of the base, examine structures and terrain currently out of your line of sight, complete your survey of the fencing, and keep your ears perked for personnel activity. Jeffrey nods as you signal to your chest, the visor, and point to the north. He signals "Ok, chief," and pats his rifle, then shows four fingers and points to the northwest portion of the foothills.

Maneuvering low and slow you position yourself close to the fencing. In the prone position you note how the northern section of the base seems to slope to a lower elevation. There are two buildings one thousand feet from your position under guard by six soldiers. Snap. You assume weapons and ammunition. Steadily making your way north you arrive at a break in the fencing. The upper portion of the northern end of the base tapers off into a point: grasslands and paved concrete ending at the base of a large creek bed, numerous rivulets fingering the entire northern end of the valley that juts into the foothills. There is no fencing for this entire portion of the northern perimeter. Entry point. Snap.

The stomach crawl to a northwestern perch in the foothills takes ninety minutes. According to the Lensicon you are one and seven tenths of a mile from the last patch of concrete at the northern edge of base. A book in a friend's bathroom once told you a thirty-nine year old Toronto man holds the Guinness World Record for fastest mile crawl: twenty-three minutes forty-five seconds. Triton could have used him. With over an hour until you reconvene with Jeffrey you decide to rest your eyes instead of observing the skeleton crew guarding the base at 0427. Pressed against the foothills in full ghillie camouflage you take slow breaths of that oxygen rich atmosphere. Crickets.

You are falling backwards in a black vacuum, the only noise is the whipping of your clothing in the frigid wind. You're having trouble turning over, the unseen force pulls you down. You can't breathe.

"Get a grip, you're going to compromise us."

Jeffrey has his hand over your mouth. He points up and you increase elevation to observe the base from the northwest during these final hours of your mission. Small groups of soldiers are up for their morning run. Snap. Lights are on in less than a third of the buildings. Wide angle snap. You take a few more images of the vehicle lots to ensure the correct GPS data is recorded. You draw on some water and scribble in your notebook until reveille pierces the soundless ether. 0800. Documenting the morning routine you have confirmed there are less than three hundred soldiers operating this base. Jeffrey snaps the titanium bipod against his barrel, slaps you on the shoulder, and moves in a hunch through the oaks. You hike west and link back with the paved mountain road.

Touching down at the Triton compound, Mallory and Peter are waiting at the helipad. Mallory is expressionless holding the padded camera case before her; once the Lensicon is placed in the foam cradle Mallory snaps it shut and trots off. Two servants assist you and Jeffrey in the disrobing of your ghillie suits. Two more handle Jeffrey's rifle and sub-machine gun, as well as your notebooks and pack. Peter is beaming. Gripping you each by the outside shoulder he exclaims:

"'It is a rough road that leads to the heights of greatness!' Do you know Seneca? The American people owe you a debt of gratitude. Your information is on its way to logistics as we speak. Let's celebrate! Clean up, take a siesta, and come by the house at say… a little before happy hour, if you can manage."

Walking to barracks your thoughts turn to Martin Luther King Jr.:

"Faith is taking the first step even when you don't see the whole staircase."

Will your intentions manifest truth and goodness? Every day you think of the rose garden.

9

Peter Triton is manhandling a Taylor Grand Symphony twelve string guitar: an awkward hand fumbles along the ebony fingerboard, abalone and mother of pearl would snicker if they could, the koa wood body sings an unknown song as it rests on his thigh.

"Mallory, sweet Mallory, you certainly earn that salary, Mallory I'd marry you, if it weren't for damn legality."

"Smashing, Peter. You've really missed your calling."

Mallory nods to you as she escapes the inebriated minstrel. She is conservatively dressed in a flowing green dress. Examining the ballroom inhabitants: Scottish wool of the highest thread count exchanging odd handshakes, men you've never seen, a woman draped in a pink cape. You feel like a sore thumb in your fatigues until you catch the simultaneous smile, point, and wink hovering above a shot glass of clear liquid. Down the hatch, Jeffrey walks behind Mallory and tugs at the back of her hair before approaching you.

"Fashionably late. They've been getting after it. Refreshments flown in."

The center of the ballroom is occupied by a trident shaped table with settings along the outside and a solitary setting at the end of the center section. Sticky rice, mango, cherries and berries, coconut mousse, crispy chicken, Vietnamese mint, soft shell crab and cilantro, pork and pickled carrots, salmon sashimi, dark red cuts of tuna, pink slabs of tuna, and scallops; an entire smorgasbord of cultures fusing atop a three pronged table. Instead of a formal seating arrangement the guests are roaming around the ballroom picking at plates and draining glass or flute. Peter rests the guitar against the wall and walks your way, flicking a piece of meat from the silver platter, chewing with satisfaction as he smiles and speaks from the unoccupied portion of his mouth.

"Horse meat. Basashi. I see an empty pair of hands, may I trouble you old sport?!"

Peckwith steps from behind an elaborate bar cart, his forearm draped with fine linen:

"Yes, sir."

"Open a 2006 Domaine de la Romanée-Conti. If my friend sees the bottom of a glass before that bottle is finished you will find yourself at the whipping post."

"Very good."

"Taking a break from Triton Vineyards and fresh California game?"

"My friend, my friend. The grand design is coming to fruition. When it was time to act, you did indeed act. Do you not realize the gravity? Our capability, our fortitude, these are no longer mysteries, the first step of the long journey is behind us."

The slap of a Kodiak thuds into the center of your spine. Jeffrey has his arm around your shoulder.

"No doubt, Pete. That's why we spent months separating the artists from the pretenders. When it's time to jump, we gonna jump."

Jeffrey unleashes a wolf howl, with his reared head he is indifferent to the curious looks from the remainder of the salon. Instant clarity confirms Peter is approaching intoxication and there are reasons Jeffrey restricts liquor intake.

"The situation is evident, Peter. You want to take this 'fortitude' from the United States and use it against the government? You really think fifteen hundred people can take on the United States military?"

"In a sense, but you are quite far off, quite far off my friend. I am not a warlord. How did that work out in Africa? Turkey? Venezuela? No, no. This is all about leverage. We will not gun down our own countrymen, or at least we will do our part to avoid such conflict. Have patience. In a few days this brigade will devour the finest holiday meal enjoyed by anyone in some time. Christmas Day for those of our ilk, a simple celebratory feast for those on the right side of this mission. Forty-eight hours later you will receive the final briefing."

Light at the end of this tunnel.

"Look around this room. These people have shaped the world."

Peter shoos away Jeffrey and replaces the arm around your shoulder with his own.

"There is a reason you are in this room. Your actions this morning will shape the future of your city, your state, your country, your world. Look at these people, look at him there. Does that look like a man who drives through two hours of traffic to sit at a desk and hit someone else's deadlines? That man has influenced your life more than Penicillin, and you don't even know it. Influence, shaping the tide. Do you honestly think an earthquake caused the destruction of Los Angeles? You heard the seismologists lament, megathrust this and megathrust that, and then poof. What have you heard since? Where are the reports? Of course there is no money for a commission. Honestly, in this information age you have no excuse."

The cosmic conveyor belt is steadily delivering disasters, epiphanies, paradoxes, hope, fear, highs, and lows. You are not numb to the exponentially increasing phenomena, in fact the impact on your mental health is quite clear. Critical thinking, analysis, strategy, integrity, and a relentless grip on your own morality. Crystal clear, this is the only way. Joseph Campbell, "Your own path you make, with every step you take."

"You've been to Montecito, you've slept in my home. I have enough gold buried under that farm to start a new society. Some of the people in this room belong to a club that's been around longer than your granddaddy's granddaddy plus a thousand. We are prepared. We are ready."

Red, blue, and black fruits dance with spice and earth, the burgundy red washes warm over your body, and you feel the need to step away from Triton to absorb another onslaught of thought.

"Peter, do you believe in God?"

"I... I will be honest with you, I struggle with faith. I believe in me. I can tell you that. I believe in me, and what we are doing here."

Peckwith pours another glass of class as you eyeball a tray of tuna with high fat content. The tall wide man standing to your left is the third of three fatigued ballroom dwellers.

"August Pike. You can call me Gus as long as you never call me Auggie. What you did today was outstanding."

Proficient strumming tickles your ear. You turn to the pleasant surprise of Jeffrey in a gilded chair, displaying his hidden talent to the woman with the pink cape. His skill with the string allows you to recognize the brooding classic from Alice In Chains, his head bowed and voice remarkably sincere:

Forgot my woman,
Lost my friend,
Things I've done,
And where I've been,
Sleep in sweat,
The mirror's cold,
I've seen my face,
It's growing old.
Scared to death!
A reason why,
Do whatever,
To get me by,
Think about,
Things I've said,
Read the page,
It's cold and dead!
Now take me home,
Yeah,
Take me home,
Take me home,
Yeah.
Take me home.
Say goodbye,
Don't follow.

The advanced state of intoxication in this ballroom couples with your valid exhaustion. Planning your exit as you drain the final drop of DRC, you excuse yourself to the restroom and escape the colonial mansion without detection. Walking the grounds you marvel at the amount of effort and planning required to yield such a campaign. A hive of activity under half a moon at dinner time on Wednesday. Fifty-eight seat charter buses are lined up at the gate waiting to be cleared for entrance. A procession of catering staff feeds into the auditorium. Small groups of fatigues walk and talk with the social comfort of a university campus. Vintage Broncos gurgle up and down smooth pavement, merriment escapes the open door of a building. Oblivious? No. Fulfilled? Maybe. Dangerous? Yes. This certainly beats that commute Triton referenced. The masses stuffed into their metal coffins, corralled up and down the 405, tapping away on their phones when they should be driving, calling people sheep on social media without turning that brutal mirror.

Your room appears empty as you look at Brubaker's section and veer right, until you notice Grommet standing silently before Catherine's vacant bunk. He is running his fingers over the embroidered patch of a stoic bearded fisherman casting his net across the state of California.

"Do you think she'd be proud of me?"

"Don't you mean impressed? I don't know Grommet, I barely knew her and she's not here."

"I heard you and Jeffrey did something real today. We are in motion."

Looking out the window, rubbing his emblem, in his own existential crisis we call the human condition.

"I'll let you rest. Hey, I'd like to sit with you at Christmas dinner. Is that ok with you? I'm Buddhist."

"Of course."

Wandering towards what should be another nightmare laden dreamscape, your attention is refocused to the present as a shrill howl slices through the compound, followed by the giggles of two women. Laughing, you burrow the base of your skull into the goose down pillow.

10

Ginger brined turkey, coffee crusted beef tenderloin, roasted
garlic potatoes, spinach dripping with strawberry vinaigrette,
ham drizzled in glaze, game hens topped with olives and
capers, boeuf en croûte, pecan pork with Parmesan, croissant,
éclair, opera cake, mille-feuille, silver spoons floating on
clouds of whipped cream, macarons, browned butter carrots
and cauliflower, candied butternut squash, roast baby beets,
drip coffee, spring water, espresso, wine, and cognac laced
egg nog. Who's got it better than us?

Seated between Jeffrey and Grommet you are eager to bypass
whatever speech Triton is preparing, as he stands alone
onstage beside a standing microphone and linen draped
table. Arms folded, playing with his belt, shuffling the
notecards on the table, looking around, Triton is allowing the
room to fill, working the anticipation to feverish heights.
Jeffrey is rubbing his palms together and smiling. Grommet
keeps nudging you with his elbow and pointing at elaborate
dessert trays.

The auditorium is full, only a few on the far ends are securing
their seats. The air is stale, too much respiration, and the
mumbling conversations have bottlenecked any auditory
senses that would decipher actual language. Your mind keys
in on the sound of heavy silver napkin rings slumping onto
the ground, or maybe a silver paper weight.

An explosive, concussive force appears fully formed in less
than an instant. You are airborne and conscious enough to

realize none of your body parts are touching the floor. The bang felt like four fists striking your head on all sides in one moment, a delivery truck catching you running a red light on your bike. Floating backwards you witness the thick cypress table tops flying up to meet you, bending end over end while bodies summersault upwards, offering limb and plasma to the mélange of pure chaos. On your back atop a pile of squirming torsos, you watch the feast suspend just long enough to remind you of its existence, before falling to the ground in a slap of ruined protein and jangle of silverware. The cypress table tops clack against the ground, sending tremors into the earth as they end their crushing dance.

Fear. Confusion. Panic. Sights that will never be unseen. The stage left section of the auditorium has become pockets of anguishing human, debris, and shell-shocked bystanders. A man with his wits intact realizes this is a crisis situation, as he stands to move towards one of the table craters he is cut to shreds by a wall of barking machine guns. The auditorium is under an advancing line of automatic gunfire. Kicking up bits of flesh, wood, and food as you taste copper in your mouth. Jeffrey's body is pushed forcefully against your own. Another rage of gunfire erupts, but there are no ricocheting bullets or piles of liquid pulp flying about your field of view. A blinding light lances your brain, another concussive force rings your skull, and the sustained automatic gunfire extends into one long rip of thick paper.

Silence. Blindness. Pushing weight off your chest and legs. Gunpowder stings the lungs and eyes. Blurry vision and ringing ears. Triton prone on the stage under a seven man pyramid. No more gunshots. Security kicking weapons away from bodies. You look nearby at Jeffrey lying on his back with his gaze fixed on you. You lean forward, the instinct is to grab him at the chest by his fatigues and pull him to his feet, only in reality chunks of his shoulder and torso are missing. The ground is covered in his blood, and blood from so many around you. Never averting his gaze, he reaches out with his right hand and grips your shoulder with substantial force. You have no words for this situation, all you can do is live in it, be there. The strength gripping your shoulder, face to face, his eyes with the desperate joy of a steer that somehow escaped the slaughterhouse, embracing a final trot down the road in a city he's never seen, not looking back towards his inevitable captors. The eyes do not waver, the grip loosens and falls.

You run your hands across your entire body. All limbs are present, your hands are black and shiny with dirt and blood. You force your body to stand, the dark fatigues clothing the motionless do not give much indication of wound location. The attackers reveal themselves as you impulsively shuffle towards the exit. Kalashnikovs, AR-15s, and SCAR rifles have been kicked away from stationary attackers with sucking chest wounds and missing limbs. They are wearing grey pajamas, or uniforms. All of them. Examining each face, confused, you realize you should be helping people, not leaving. You move towards piles of injured cohorts. Pausing for a moment while stepping over a pajama clad assailant, your stomach drops to the floor when you realize Catherine is lying in a pool of blood at your feet, mouth frozen in a scream, eyes wide open, unmistakable. Who are these people? Us. The dissenters. How long has it been, what have they been doing to them? The logistical genius is crumpled in a pile of unanimated meat.

Five people in white coats storm into the auditorium. Are five doctors the extent of the medical personnel responsible for this entire compound? One of them shouts she is a trauma surgeon. One, while the other four tend to a victim each. Peter Triton is stomping amongst the chaos and berating the security team.

"How could this happen?!"

One of the doctors looks up from his work.

"Peter, we are not equipped for this, not even close. These people need medical evacuation. We'll begin loading the gurneys, how many helicopters are available?"

"You know we can't involve the public!"

"Peter, we have four general practitioners and one surgeon!"

"Do what you can! Everyone, if you see bleeding, stop it, apply bandages and maintain pressure on the wound. You, you, you, get extra bodies in here. You, take twenty men and bring all the medical supplies you can carry. You, get a group together and coordinate triage outside of this building. Security, sweep the base. You men, follow me to the command center."

Groaning and squirming bodies. Only five tables suffered explosions, but the damage is extensive. There are large portions of the hall that have been untouched by bullets, unshaken by whatever explosive devices were implemented. The men and women from these tables are tending to the victims, or raising their arms until a doctor can advise action, a surreal spread of holiday cheer untouched along cypress table tops, the finest feast you'll ever witness and no one touched so much as a drumstick.

Brubaker is pressing a wet clump of napkin into a bullet wound. Grommet is standing beside him, weeping and covered in blood and filth with his hand raised. You move outside and begin assisting with triage configuration. The loudspeaker repeats:

"This is an emergency situation. Report to your company commanders. This is an emergency situation."

Eventually the victims with hopes of survival have been carried to the medical facility, less and more serious victims are spread about cots under makeshift tenting. You are seated beside a man who is not going to make it. Holding his hand, you press bandages into a gaping hole at his ribs. Similar to Jeffrey's wounds. Jeffrey. You don't have a company commander. It was just you and Jeffrey. They're going to have to take the S off your emblem.

Holding the man's hand you are not positive he is still alive, but you hold on, half as a provisional measure and half from shock. Fanaticism. Hypocrisy. Forcibly detained, could they have escaped? It would be difficult to get out of this compound, but they managed to acquire weapons, why not acquire a vehicle and flee? Hike off into the mountains. They killed your friend and you hate them for it. Rage. You despise the notion of internment despite logic noting surprise and secrecy are crucial. What disgusting scenes play out between contradicting groups of humans.

"Security threat neutralized. Report to your company commanders. Security threat neutralized."

He's gone. You're holding a cold compress against the forehead of a woman who caught a bullet in the boot. She is screaming for morphine, which is in abundance, but you have no idea how to dose this out. Holding her down, yelling at a doctor, he tells you to stick one in her thigh and squeeze. Checking her tourniquet, pressing the compress, you hold her hand. Dozens dead, dozens wounded. This won't stop fifteen hundred people from the mission. Senseless killing.

Hours later you are showered and sitting on your trunk, aching in mental anguish and physical agony from declining any opiate. Miraculously you have avoided shrapnel and bullet. Brubaker is there, comatose. Someone trashed Catherine's bunk and no one in this room or on this floor has the energy to address such a futile act. The barracks are full of silent humans more mortal than they were this morning. Loudspeaker:

"Ladies and gentlemen, this is Peter Triton. My heart is with you. We will not let the actions of psychotics derail our undertaking. Final briefing has been moved to 1600 tomorrow afternoon. Take what you need to sleep. Mallory is coordinating grief counseling and crisis management here at the command center, all are welcome. No assignments tomorrow, meet with your company commanders at 1400 and be back in the auditorium at 1600. I am here for you."

Waking in the late morning, you lie in bed, breathing. Brubaker's bunk is squared away. In your mini-fridge there is a Tupperware of slow roasted rabbit and two Heinekens. Slowly chewing the seasoned meat you tilt back a dram of ice cold lager: chewing, another swig. You stand and step into your fatigues. Gesturing the second bottle, you nod and crack it open, leaning it sideways, high noon sunbeams refracting through green glass and bubbling liquid, glugging from the bottleneck, foaming on the tigerwood.

While you slept someone undertook the Herculean effort of transporting the dead and wounded from triage to medical, as well as clearing thousands of pounds of cypress, food waste, and shrapnel from the auditorium. The floors of the great hall have been scrubbed down, the only remnants of yesterday are sad black starbursts graffitied in a ghostly diagram. Well over one thousand sets of fatigues stand at attention. An aide fishes you out of the crowd and instructs you to sit onstage beside Mallory and Pike. Peter Triton appears from behind the curtain and steps center stage at a quick pace, foregoing any theatrics, cutting to the chase.

"Words cannot describe the atrocity we all experienced. Yes, the cat is out of the bag, these people that we recruited to work among us, these people were being detained. I think the logic is pretty clear why we didn't put them on a Greyhound back home, yes? Is that any excuse to murder dozens of innocent people? To honor our dead we need to focus on the reason we are here. We are here for the families that can't feed their kids, for the eighty year old woman that can't find part time work to pay for her husband's medicine, for the man that was down on his luck until he found himself homeless with nowhere to turn because his only living family member is incarcerated for life. We are here to return unalienable rights. To ensure the proper delivery of the final briefing I proudly hand the stage to a man with military experience, August Pike."

The curtain is fully drawn and reveals the activated screen behind the stage. You lean from your seat to see it display the same map of California used in Mallory's briefing.

"Listen up! This is a special operation. Put your specialized training to use and have faith the rest of us are doing our job. We are going to minimize the frictions of war by keeping it simple. Through surprise and speed we will achieve relative superiority. Here are the broad strokes. 2200 on December 30th our Silent Darkness Cyberwarfare companies will cut power to Fort Bowman. Winged Sentinels and Hundred-Handers will enter the base and achieve relative superiority the second they get one of those Apaches in the air. We will secure the vehicles, weapons, and ammunition, then link up north with Tower Overlord companies from the Triton compound. Highway Cerberus companies will shut down transportation for anyone we don't want following us.

Convoy en route to San Francisco, we will maintain control over Fort Bowman until the convoy arrives in San Francisco. Upon arrival we will commandeer San Francisco International Airport and secure the southern transportation arteries into the city. Remaining personnel at Fort Bowman will take the C-130s to SFO. Setting a perimeter from Hunters Point to Lake Merced, Lands End to Embarcadero, we will fortify the city of San Francisco."

Stunned silence. Triton struts forth shaking his fist.

"This is William Wallace taking Northern England!"

"What's to stop Edwards Air Force Base from scrambling jets and bombing our convoy?"

Pike puffs his chest, "Maybe the AH-64 Apache attack helicopter, with the ability to hover in place, do backflips and barrel rolls, sling laser guided Hellfire missiles or dozens of rockets, and cut down trees with a 30 mm chain gun. You'll have about two and a half hours of Apache escort, son."

Triton raises his finger, "More importantly, every person in this room is a citizen of the United States. That still means something. Imagine a scenario where the United States military unleashes aggression towards United States citizens standing on American soil? You think they're stretched pretty thin right now? Imagine angry citizens picking up one of the three hundred million guns that are already spread across this country."

Mallory slicks back her black hair and brushes some behind her ears, smiling while her diamond earrings play with the light until the moment they draw back into her mane.

"They may have some heavy weaponry, but they're not the only ones. Militias have grown exponentially since the days of eight man groups skipping showers out in the woods. Hell, there are three militias operating around Humboldt as I speak. No, the government can be called many names but stupid is not one of them. This operation is a means to get our voices heard. When I set up command I will brief the media, let the people of San Francisco know they are not in danger, and then talk to the president, and let me tell you, the president will listen."

"What about the police?"

Triton laughs. "The police? San Francisco is the financial center of the west coast, maybe the technology center of the world, and a western headquarters for this little gentlemen's club I belong to. The police are taken care of, and let me tell you, let me tell you old sport, it cost not ten percent of that Klimt I bought last month. Much, much less, and really what would you do walking the beat as a supposed public servant when an Abrams tank turns the corner? The police, he says."

Pike adjusts his fatigues.

"That's everything in a nutshell. You've got three days to do whatever you want as long as you are bright eyed and bushy tailed when we execute. Run through light training. I don't want any hangovers. Help your fellow man and woman with what we saw here last night. Now, if you don't want to be involved in this endeavor that is fine! Just remain in this room as everyone leaves. You will be treated with respect."

Fields of gold untilled in limbo. What would yield from the work of your hands? Who would benefit? Thinking of baby Lyle in your arms, head bobbing from your chest to the occasional stare into your eyes as he clutches your shoulder. What is deserved? What type of world is shaping him, what environment welcomes him into existence, what will it mean to be a man when he becomes one?

11

The dim tube is silent save the stressed engine and overmatched transmission; you and fifty of your closest friends quietly rumble upon fuzz balls that attempt to distort a hypnotic pattern of blue, purple, and pink cloth. The trek through these mountains and their fire roads might be as harrowing as the mission. For almost one mile you peer out the window at a one thousand foot drop, uneasy since the moment a front passenger wheel lipped off a dusty dirt rock edge. Brake lights cast a red glow against the rocks and form spindly shadow monsters above the vegetation. The majority of the bus is alternating between their naked eye and Sightmark SM15070 Ghost Hunter 1x24 night vision goggles. A recording of August Pike cuts into the hum and repeats twice.

"Take the field. Carry out the mission at all cost."

Grommet extends his gloved fists forward as if he was preparing to swing from a trapeze. His face is mostly goggle, save long black hair and a big white smile. Rows of people sit at keyboards and LED computer monitors and stare at Grommet as he maintains his pose in front of a large satellite image overlay of California. Small collections of green dots blink across the entire state. Drawing a breath Grommet extends both thumbs horizontally; as he exhales he turns them towards the ground. With this, Silent Darkness tap their keys and unleash a torrent of ones and zeros.

California power companies are now victim to multiple unauthorized takeovers of command programs. Employees stand from their chairs in disbelief and watch the mouse move itself, unresponsive to their own hand, as it clicks off each substation's individual transformers and power lines. Malware is activated to destroy their automation software. These transformers will have to be switched on by human hand at the substation. Salinas to San Luis Obispo, Bakersfield to Fresno, one by one the little green dots in this area blink red.

"Get Tower snipers to shoot up the San Luis Obispo and Bakersfield substations. We don't want them coming back on."

Walking as quietly as five hundred pairs of boots can walk, you are in formation along a familiar paved road. You adjust the straps that secure the revolver, you examine the ghillie suit camouflage foliage. There is no real chain of command with this group, instructions are to act as a swarm and achieve the clear goals laid out during briefing. You and Brubaker seem to have the respect of your fellow crusaders, due to your visible interaction with the higher ups, and you feel like something of a team captain. Influential in spirit and one of their own. You are also one of five being shadowed by radiomen connected directly to Triton and the command center. Everyone spreads out and begins creeping through nature, off the pavement and towards the steep drop into the creek bed.

Half of the base is pitch black, and the southern half of the base is lit up like a Christmas tree. Solar power. That was in the images. What a foolish mistake. The soldiers on base have been alerted by a premature and incompletely manufactured power failure. The buzzing pizza pie of a perfect full moon laughs from the heavens. Still, the northern half of the base is at a disadvantage, and the creek bed is in as much darkness as moonlight will allow. Guard facilities in this half of the base are shining most of their one hundred eighty degrees of spotlight southward. Night vision activated, restricted to hand signals, you head the pack as a swarm of black and brown curls down the foothills and into the soggy creek. The water is cold but clear during your chin deep creek crawl. The squirming organisms behind you sound like flopping fish.

"Time to make it do what it do," whispers Brubaker.

You signal the visor and begin shepherding a platoon sporting the Winged Sentinel emblem, crawling inside the base along the western perimeter of the fencing. Pausing for a moment you examine the western guard shack a few hundred feet from the perimeter. Two guards are sweeping spotlights along the air strip, and one guard has placed three rifles against the wall while he slaps the metallic sides of communication equipment. You roll onto your side and look one thousand meters to the northeast, using your goggles to assess the flock of little green men dashing through the darkness and kneeling beside Abrams tanks, the lone spotlight in that area slumped towards the pavement directly in front of the guard tower.

A sound like someone throwing a fistful of quarters against a railing, and the spitting of a carnival gun cutting paper corners off a playing card, you look back to the shack and see puffs of dark vapor and snapping panes of glass while three men fall into twitching clumps. One of the platoon looks at you with wide eyes that say without saying:

"Did you really think we'd get through this without killing anyone?"

The Winged Sentinels run hunched towards the Apaches, and in quick succession have popped the canopies on all of the aircraft, strapping themselves in and either getting acquainted with an old friend or touching physical controls for the first time outside of a simulator. In the distance you can hear the telltale sound of a turbine engine powering up the Abrams. The radio clicks on.

"Run it."

Seconds later the chop chop chop of an AugustaWestland comes into earshot. Taking a knee you peer beyond the tree line to the south and spy one of Triton's choppers descending towards the main road entrance. A pyrotechnic display commences as flashing washes out your display, the software in your goggles automatically adjusts to the chaff and flare countermeasures rocketing from both sides of the AugustaWestland as the aircraft dives then rears back, the pintle-mounted Browning M3M machine gun pelting heavy lead into the terracotta with a force you can feel through the ground. The nose lurches up as the aircraft banks and dips, climbing quickly and moving south to escape or perhaps chart another diversionary attack sweep. Automatic rifle fire pops in the open air and small spark showers glow bright behind the AugustaWestland. The muzzle flares flash sporadically from some of the northern buildings, a portion of the official barracks section to the south, and a heavy concentration from the auxiliary barracks just outside of the fencing in the hills to the east of the base.

The collective turbine whoosh has been joined by the clanging procession of squeaking tank treads. The M1 Abrams have released their smokescreens, a thick mist hovers like a vertical raincloud dividing the base. Each tank driver processes the one hundred twenty degree field of view provided by three night vision equipped periscopes. The Abrams have formed a horizontal line segment across the entire base, the post office and hotel complex exist mutely at the midpoint, room lights briefly flick on and quickly return to darkness. Multiple rifles crack automatic fire from the third story of a Spanish style building on the northeastern section of the base. A turret silently swivels as you watch a Hundred-Hander man the up top .50 caliber machine gun: a rapid thumping of chunky gunfire disintegrates plaster and splinters the wood, tile, and furniture into the surrounding scenery, essentially ripping the entire third story from the Spanish style dwelling.

Two General Electric turboshaft engines whir to life as the Apache nearest you powers up. You are prone in the tall grass as your radioman rises to a hunched crouch and runs a thousand feet to the east. On his loudspeaker he begins to repeat:

"Stand down. You are outgunned. Stand down. You will not be fired upon. We are American. Stand down. You will not be fired upon. Stand down."

Cracking asphalt leaps upwards, cutting into the flesh of his face. The radioman narrowly escapes a strafing of NATO 5.56 by rolling and scurrying to his left behind a metal shipping container. Ricochets are kicking up cement near the whirring Apache. The pilot disengages the blade locks as the rotors begin to move and hastily increase speed. Rifle fire in this immediate vicinity comes to an eerie halt as the buzzing chop of the Apache blade lifts the aircraft with the whirring power of twin turbines. The idling tanks one thousand meters in the distance are drowned out by the hissing hover of the rising Apache, wet blades of long grass whipping into your face while vegetation is pressed into the ground and dust is kicked into cloudy hurricanes. The lone airborne Apache is yawing towards the main barracks in an intimidating hover. Rifle fire has ceased. You see a green man disengage from one of the Abrams and run to the front of an idle infantry company.

"On me," shouts Brubaker, waving his hand in three exaggerated sweeps.

He places his hand on his throat and points at three sections of the company, assigning each group an area of buildings to secure. The Apache hovers and banks, gaining altitude. Boot rubber clods and echoes off pavement as Hundred-Handers storm buildings, with your night vision goggles you see the white outlines of zip ties bouncing against their belts. The hotel complex is completely ignored. Cawing crows reconfigure their treetop positions as the Apache is slowly orbiting the base. Boots pound on stairs and overturned furniture bangs against floor and wall, shouting and confusion, a hovering hiss in and out of earshot. The grounds are randomly littered with lifeless shapes draped in different uniforms.

The tanks begins forming a vertical line at the north end of the base. Hundred-Handers are firing up the Stryker armored fighting vehicles, Bradley fighting vehicles, Humvees, cargo trucks, and even forklifts. The rumble of a low grade earthquake skulks in from the northern hills. Your interest is piqued considering this lasted longer than a minute and featured the upsetting moan of twisting metal. Beckoning your radio man you call for a report from anyone with information.

"Triton here! Absolutely loving what I am seeing! That was ten charter buses being driven off the side of a mountain. Don't worry about it, we never figured out a way to turn them around on a fire road, and we damn sure don't want anyone using them when we're gone. Armored convoy is going to take the main road out of Dodge. We're going to have the freeways nice and open for everyone. If anybody needs the road we took in, that's an option too. Love what you're doing, bubby. You should see me right now, I'm doing the electric slide over here. Pike and Mallory can't recognize panache."

Whimpering electric motors propel carts carrying rockets and Hellfire missiles to four naked Apaches. When the Apache twin turbine is at the far end of its orbit you notice the distinct whir of five quadcopter drones. Walking the distance to the C-130s you wave a Sentinel into the cockpit to open the cargo ramp and door. The whine of machinery and hydraulics split the tail in half, the door folding upwards and the ramp extending towards the concrete. You can fit four Humvees and fifty soldiers in each plane. There are only two C-130s on the ground this evening. The missing third plane you reconnoitered with Jeffrey has earned zero concern because a drone is buzzing two feet from your head, and swiveling its camera before you grab it with both hands and smash it propeller side down onto the pavement, thrusting your GSG9 through the aggravating construct of carbon fiber and wiring.

Over one hundred heavily armored high powered assault vehicles head south towards the two lane highway and presumably the 101 north. Half of the Abrams break off from the rear and accelerate at impressive speed towards the front of the convoy. The twin turbines of four more Apache helicopters start their song. You're standing upright under a suit of grass and shrubbery, playing your part in a civil war bathed in silver light. We almost made it two hundred years.

Officer Morales is struggling in the dark on the corner of 3rd St and Ellis St, King City, California. Having ushered a woman and her nine year old son into a residence, he flashes his Maglite towards a large bearded blacksmith of a man wildly gesturing his clenched hands from forehead to belly button in double half-moon flexes.

"Action Jackson had to do the night burn, man! Power is out to half the state! I've been keeping my motor clean all week, I need to get Tyler home while I can, before I—"

Bending down to rip two fists full of grass, the man is pounding his chest.

"Shelley get in the house I pay for! Look, officer, I had to get him up here now, I have big plans for the New Year. It's four hours back to L.A., man."

"I had plans too! You were supposed to be here tomorrow afternoon!"

"Ma'am, please remain indoors."

The small town neighborhood glows under a layer of central California fog backlit by maximum moon. This radiance is emphasized by a residential zone completely void of electricity. Stars glimmer in a pool of Tyrian purple. A Ford F150 in the distance silhouettes Action Jackson as he jukes right and lunges left around the officer, towards the house. Officer Morales tackles the man to the concrete with a meaty thud. Strapping handcuff to wrist he asks Shelley to take Tyler and stay with a friend or family member in case Action Jackson makes bail tonight.

"Morales."

Chief is running communications powered by station generators.

"Morales. I need you to cut the freeway both directions at 1st St. Now."

"Chief, I've got a—"

"Now, Morales... and Morales, if you see anything you can't handle, remove yourself from the equation. Do you understand me? Go to Gia's for the night."

"Chief."

Removing his knee from a back soaked in Jack Daniels infused sweat, Morales gets to his feet and begins the half block walk back to his cruiser. He is completely baffled by the widespread power outage and cryptic orders. This is not how he wanted New Year's Eve to begin.

"So what, fine, Chief wants me to move, Chief can deal with that handcuffed madman from Los Angeles."

Morales hears the dual exhausted gargle of an American V8 sparking to life. That must be Action Jackson's Petty blue Mustang that was parked across the lawn, soon to be someone else's problem in someone else's precinct. He probably looped his cuffed hands under his legs. It should be tough driving a manual wearing bracelets. The exhaust notes of the V8 trail off into the purple sky while Morales banks right on 1st St towards the section that bridges the 101. Stars are so bright tonight.

Two strange helicopters surging high speed at low altitude startle Morales. Less than one mile from the freeway his eyes and ears are assaulted by a steadfast display of military might. Morales sits in awe and silence after pulling to a stop on 1st St, overlooking the 101 in both directions. Belching, thrusting, humming, trudging, and jetting up the 101 north is an armored column he can only equate to images portrayed in films of the Gulf and Iraq Wars.

"This must be a large scale military exercise. Chief needed everyone on hand and couldn't tell us why."

Morales remains in awe until the final backside of an M1 Abrams rolls up the 101 north. All cars in the immediate vicinity have backed off. Shortly, with whatever that was now in the distance, freeway traffic is starting to proliferate as the clock strikes that precarious moment thirty minutes after last call. Radio reports notified Morales that local taverns were using candles, lanterns, and cell phone flashlights to conduct cash transactions and keep the mirth flowing.

A firm foot is required on the accelerator as Morales must assert his position amongst the homeward bound nightlife revelers, swerving his cruiser from lane to lane and decelerating, cutting off traffic on the 101 north. Lights flashing, he leaves the cruiser parked horizontal on the northbound freeway, and uses a series of flares to slow and then stop traffic on the southbound portion. Angry unmoving motorists lean from their windows and huff in the parlance of Action Jackson, until Morales approaches their vehicles, and they decide to put a pane of glass between their liquored breath and the olfactory senses of an officer of the law.

"Freeway shut down both directions, Chief."

A California Highway Patrol cruiser zooms along the shoulder beside Morales, eventually parking sideways on the dirt before the trees that speckle the earth between the southbound off-ramp and the 101 itself.

"Not in the mood for your practical jokes tonight, Barrera."

Walking back to his cruiser, Morales flashes his spotlight at the highway patrol car, expecting a return sequence of light from California Highway Patrol Officer Barrera, his roadway rival and occasional pancake compatriot at V's Diner. No light. Another patrol car has arrived from the south and is parked along the patch of dirt hill between the northbound on-ramp and the 101. Headlights off.

Crickets chirp as the gasoline engines idle, hybrid vehicles switch to electronic drivetrain, and the automated electric car waits in patient silence beneath a glittering sky. The blast of a compression release engine brake cuts into the hum emanating from the sedated procession of motorists. A big rig's cold brakes are screeching, the odd rubbing noises of loose wheel covers continue to announce the eighteen wheeler's presence as the diesel engine pushes and pulls the shiny double trailer into the Exxon station on the corner of 1st St and the 101 north on-ramp.

"Big rig hauling all that gasoline is just going to make a quick stop at the small town gas station."

Morales pops the trunk and fishes out a small pair of binoculars. Leaning his hip against the rear of his vehicle he raises the suction cups to his eyes, working the focus knob. Difficult to see in the dark, but Morales can confirm that Officer Barrera is nowhere to be found, instead there are three men in dark clothing pressed against a CHP cruiser. One of the men has his face buried in some form of binocular or rangefinder and is waving with his thumb and two fingers in a mocking hello. Without removing the apparatus from his face, the man motions a big rig air horn signal. Morales thinks he can make out the hint of a smile behind the rangefinder, before muzzle flash erupts from the other two men propped against the CHP cruiser. Morales' front driver side tire explodes in a rubbery pop as what seems like a delayed boom of gunfire cracks in the distance. Another crack follows in quick succession, and Morales is scrambling to the other side of his vehicle, shielding his body against the rear wheel well. 7.62 mm bullets are tearing chunks of sheet metal off his cruiser, piercing his engine and breaking glass. The pot shots escalate to automatic gunfire, while Morales peers from underneath the body of his cruiser to see occupants fleeing their stopped vehicles as bullets render them immobile, to say the least.

Inebriated bar patrons, late night lovers, families returning from friendly visits, a sea of people spilling in all directions across December fields and dirt lots. Sparks leaping with puckish glee, glass and ripped steel litter the 101 in both directions. Morales' spotlight is still on the column of cars, he can see there are no bodies or injured motorists, and with the gunfire concentrated on inanimate objects he sprints and dives into the deep ditch separating the northbound 101 from farmland.

The mating call of the long haul trucker, a big rig air horn fills the atmosphere, the pumping diesel engine of another eighteen wheeler is throttling northwest on Mesa Verde Rd. The CHP car on the patch of dirt above the southbound freeway rips north up 1st St and donuts into a field with blue and red lights flashing. Morales notes the characteristic shiny reflection of the double tanker is muted by foam cushions strapped along both tanker tubes, the type of cushions he remembers landing on when he competed in high jump for the King City High track team.

Lacking any screeching of brakes, the big rig cuts through a dirt field instead of navigating the right turn Mesa Verde Rd takes towards 1st street. Unhindered by obviously unsafe speeds, the big rig spears between trees and barrels down the dusty hill into the southbound 101, like a run stopping middle linebacker with his helmet down, face in the fan, kicking sedans fifteen feet in the air and abruptly displacing any vehicle on the north or southbound 101 at the 1st St overpass, crunching fabricated carcasses, grinding glass, and creating an earth shattering impact as the big rig jackknifes underneath the bridge. The three remaining fatigued men are running towards the collision and duck into the maze of gnarled automotive debris.

Morales pulls himself from the ditch and hides behind a small oak tree on the outer lip of an irrigated field. Minutes later the men emerge with a fourth man. This fourth man is wearing an Explosive Ordinance Disposal suit, the thick blast suit arms draped over the shoulders of two fatigued men helping him from the wreckage. Morales can smell the gasoline and see puddling reflect moonlight. As the four men pile into the remaining cruiser they are whooping and hollering, activating the overhead blue and red lights before zipping north on 1st St to kick up farmland with their accomplices. Morales understands the reasons why he is the lone human in this square mile of California and begins to beat feet in a northwestern direction through the irrigated field.

Three steps from the seventh fairway at King City Public Golf Course, Morales is thrown face first into the ground with bullying force. A second sun has risen. Another ground quaking explosion throws a subsequent wall of heat against his beaten body. Morales shields his face to the image of a firestorm scorching acres of farmland and freeway, molten meteors that were once Volkswagens are falling back to earth like sanctuary lamps discarded from the heavens. The rust inferno licks carrot orange flames one hundred feet above the roaring barbecue that was once the 1st St overpass and 101 freeway. The overgrown flamethrower, formerly a gas station, spews conflagration. Firelight throwing shadows for miles, a black tower of smoke climbing the sky.

Grommet is conducting with aplomb, pointing to specific rows of computer jockeys. San Francisco and Sacramento plunge into darkness. Unintentionally, Los Angeles has joined her sister cities in the Stone Age. Gloved hand coyishly pressed to his giggling mouth, Grommet gestures in the motion of a cowboy signaling "round 'em up."

Triton is ecstatic. He pulls off his headset like an NFL coach that just iced the conference championship. Triton slaps Pike on the back and takes leave of the command center, arriving at the driver side of an idling, matte black Lamborghini Aventador. Mallory is waiting, strapped into the passenger seat, and the guards have already wheeled back the main gate. Coasting down the dirt road, Triton begins to sporadically punch on the accelerator, automated manual seven speed single clutch unit engaged he reflects high decibel growls off the surrounding rock face, the tri-pronged tube spewing flamethrown exhaust from the rear center of his supercar. Taxiing left onto Arroyo Seco Rd, Triton effortlessly graduates to a triple digit speedometer reading: each second they are closer to the long dark lost highway.

12

Roland Kermshep scooped a plastic bag chock-full of Grapenuts for breakfast, he placed it next to a banana earmarked for a sensible snack, and another bag stuffed to capacity with Cookie Crisp, then left all three on the kitchen counter as he whistled goodbye to his cat Merlin. The power outage had occupied too much of his brain cavity, and now his bulbous stomach is making music while he mouth breathes his way through security pat downs as a low level TSA employee.

"Belts, laptops in a separate bin, you know the drill folks."

Luckily, or unluckily depending on how much Roland enjoys sleeping in, San Francisco International Airport is one of the few complexes in the city capable of running on generators for some time. It was a mess getting to work in the early morning. Roland decides not to fathom what transportation will be like when his shift ends midday New Year's Eve.

Two soldiers shoulder sling M4A1 carbines and patrol the main entrance. One has a leash around his midsection that is connected to a Belgian Malinois. Three yellow cabs wait patiently at the curb, the drivers passionately argue while they smack their foreheads and smoke cigarettes further down the walkway. Roland has heard soldiers refer to the dog as a "Malligator." He slowly exhales and chuckles trying to imagine how far Merlin could get his plump body up the drapes if a Malinois ever burst into the apartment. Just as Roland is planning to transition from his comical masterpiece back to reality a forty thousand pound, three hundred fifty horsepower Stryker enters his field of view at fifty-one miles per hour, smashing into the leftmost taxi and creating a three car canary yellow accordion. The Stryker machine gun turret swivels to point directly at the two soldiers guarding the entrance. Both soldiers raise their hands in shock as the Malinois barks and tugs at the waist with great force. A metallic clang and the rear Stryker door has dropped, eight Sentinels feed out onto the walkway, one of them pointing his Steyr AUG directly at the soldiers.

"Hand down, man down."

Carefully circumventing the noble beast, the Sentinels have disarmed both soldiers.

"Take your dog and get out of here. We're Americans. No one is going to get hurt, and don't bother trying to leave the city. Go home and watch the morning news."

The soldiers run off as the Sentinels file through the automatic doors. Five more Strykers roll up.

"E-very-one! Flights are cancelled!"

A genuine San Francisco eccentric sashays forth to declare:

"Darling, why do I pay all this money if—"

The Steyr AUG sprays a deafening burst of automatic gunfire into the ceiling, raining asbestos on a screaming mob.

Your radio man gives you the thumbs up, SFO is under Triton control. The Stryker vehicles and their seventy mile per hour top speed will have to hold steady for the slower portion of the armored column. Your job at Fort Bowman is nearly complete. One C-130 is fully loaded with troops and four Humvees that have been crammed with computer equipment and any type of sensitive information or correspondence Triton and Pike will sift through later. You signal to the pilot and that oh so familiar turbine kicks up as the four-engine turboprop prepares to taxi.

The lone remaining Apache must have received news regarding the airport. Nose leaning forward, the body throttles north, devouring heaping helpings of altitude, no doubt nearing the minimum amount of fuel it will take to get to San Francisco.

The first C-130 is lined up for takeoff, turboprops push the plane up the runway and off the ground with surprising grace and agility for such a large aircraft. As the large rear end retreats into darkness sparks jump off the body, instantly followed by the thunder of rifles. A man running towards your position catches hot lead with his chest, spinning like a top, squashing into an unnatural position on the pavement depicting a sure loss of life. The one expense Triton spared seems to be body armor.

No one secured buildings outside of the fenced perimeter.

Fort Bowman soldiers are treating the auxiliary barracks as if it was their own private California Alamo, yet fifty well-armed civilians could never equate to fifteen hundred Mexican soldiers, and once the Fort Bowman hostages wiggle out of their zip ties the tables will turn.

You throw four smoke grenades behind the hangar, shouting for everyone to load up. Your radioman grabs you by the elbow and informs you a small team needs to return from the armory at the north of the base. The Fort Bowman soldiers are excellent marksmen, picking off black and brown fatigues that stray outside the concealing curtain of smoke. Towards the north end of the base you see a Humvee with three Hundred-Handers hanging off the doors, towing some form of trailer platform. A Fort Bowman soldier is hopping on two zip tied feet, hands fastened behind his back, when he jumps in the air and loops his hands under aerial boots, and shuffles to collect a rifle resting against a lifeless pile of fatigues.

The Humvee has arrived, hauling a wheeled platform covered in quilted moving pads. As the Humvee lines up with the C-130 ramp you pull the pads back. A polished orange tube, thirty feet long and almost four feet wide, metal wings jutting from the back third.

"What is this?"

"GBU-43. Massive Ordnance Air Blast. Eleven kilotons."

"For what?! Not on this plane."

"Triton said—"

Your palm slaps rubber butt, stainless steel released from its leather prison, seven shots ring out like cannon fire, platform and vehicle tires rendered to formless black gum and bent honeycomb metal. You holster the revolver, hook your arm into the cargo netting, and signal the flight team.

"On or off."

Thrumming engines kick into high gear. The C-130 is airborne while the cargo ramp and door struggle to close, courtesy of shot machinery. The airstrip and base shrinking into a vacuum, snapping pops of muzzle fire volley plinking lead into the aircraft body. Arm linked with the cargo netting, you release a deep sigh of relief, entire body still aching from Christmas dinner.

Nicholas is asleep in the front seat as his screen bounces fuzzy colors off the glove compartment. His father shook him out of bed with news that their hotel will accommodate a ludicrously early check in. Nicholas doesn't know his father planned this to have him there the second St. Francis Fountain opens, and after as many milkshakes as the boy can put down, they'll take a drive across the Golden Gate Bridge. His father always goes out of his way to make sure he feels special on his unfortunately timed birthday.

Nicholas' father felt the power outage could actually be to their advantage, and although it got hairy dodging the merrymakers of Santa Cruz up the 17, he has never seen the Junipero Serra Freeway so open. There hasn't been another car for five minutes. They were making incredible time.

Blue and red lights flash on the horizon. Both directions, must be a bad accident. Confusion greets him as he slows to a coast, the flashing lights are not on the freeway but on embankments and blocking the on-ramps. Concerned with the safety of his boy the man pulls to the shoulder and calls out to the officers, until he can see these are not men and women with radios and night sticks, these are three armed demons in dark clothing. Chirruping insects suddenly cease their twitter, a dull roar is growing. Fear squeezes his heart with the need to leave. At this point in time these are the badlands. The man fumbles with his seatbelt as he returns to the driver's seat. The boy awakens.

"Dad?"

The roar is no longer dull. The automatic transmission on his 2004 Oldsmobile Alero has long forgotten the intricate dance of shifting gears, but he is creating distance between them and the flashing lights. His eyes are glued to the driver's side mirror when the boy slaps his arm.

"Dad! Watch out!"

An Abrams tank is cruising forty-five miles per hour down the center of Interstate 280 with absolutely no lighting system engaged. Behind that tank is another tank, and another. The boy is flabbergasted at the sight of a forty year old man with

male pattern baldness and a five o'clock shadow hanging off
the side of a tank and sneering at him through a pane of glass.
His father veers back to the shoulder as the armored convoy
maintains course. Following the tanks are two and a half ton
cargo trucks with blinding high beam headlights, their open
beds full of people in dark clothing.

Pulling the Oldsmobile back to the shoulder the man skids
the car to a stop. He is overwhelmed by the noise, the glaring
headlights; clear danger has stoked his primal responses,
kicking open the driver door he grabs his son and pulls him
from the car. There is no end in sight to the northbound
convoy. The man almost collapses as he carries his son over
the divider and across the empty southbound freeway.
Instinct draws them into the trees, away from the marauders.

"Dad! My screen! You left my screen in the—"

He carries the boy deeper into the forest until he feels safe.
Then they watch.

The C-130 door and ramp remain open as you slough off
your ghillie suit and attach a line to the carabiner on your rig.
Your ghillie suit whips and contorts into the vortex as you
offer it to the black sky, it will probably wash up onshore for
some lucky vagrant. You survey the terrain with feet
shoulder width and firmly planted. The plane is just off the
coast bearing north as two F/A-18 Super Hornets scream
across the sky. California is an expanse of rolling black hills,
colossal scattered bonfires providing the only sources of light.
Smoke signals. This must be what the mothers and fathers of

this land would witness if they climbed a redwood one thousand years ago. The Salinan, the Yokuts, Esselen, Chalon, Rumsen, Mutsun, Awaswas, Tamyen, Ramaytush, Chochenyo, Karkin, and Miwok. For one night in 2020 California returns to the cradle.

There is no way to be sure, but you suppose this is Monterey Bay gliding out of view below. The radioman displays incredibly poor balance as he slow steps to your position, handing you the receiver.

"Top o' the world, ma! Just got to headquarters. What a view. How you looking?"

"Electricity seems to be out statewide. We had casualties on both sides. Highway Cerberus has accomplished their mission."

"Oh, yes. I can see from here. The 101, 280, the 5, the 80, 880, 680, 580, if there's an 80 you ain't driving it. They'll have the electricity restored any minute, but those roads and freeways will be out of commission for days. They tell me the Abrams just got here. We are fortifying the city. Mallory and I are setting up the command center. Mallory! Send out that EBS cell phone thing: tell them we are Americans, tell them if they live in the city and work in the city they may go about their business unhindered by us, and that we encourage them to do so, and tell them that no one can leave or enter San Francisco, and let them know we're going to be here for a while. Get the newspapers, get the morning news, and get the damn president."

While Peter barks orders and holds you hostage on the receiver your drifting eye catches an ominous sight. An outsized silver grey ship is cruising off the coast at thirty-three knots.

"Whoa. That's a Ticonderoga class warship. No joke, dude. No joke."

The man with former naval experience sits back against the fuselage, holding up his hands as if to say:

"Just sayin'."

"Peter, we encountered two jets that did not engage. We are currently north of Monterey Bay and there is a naval warship navigating the coast. Kelly says it is a Ticonderoga."

"Impossible! Wipe the muck out of your eyes, do the math. Inconceivable. Look, land that bird and get to Montgomery and Washington. Forty-eighth floor. Triton, out."

The floodlights of the airport, the blinking runway patterns, the shine of modernity is in stark contrast to the surrounding obscure blackness. Tires squeak and squelch white smoke despite the wet runway. The C-130 taxis to a rest beside her sister aircraft and two Apache helicopters. The sheer silence of the international airport injects a calmness into your soul, this is the antithesis of air travel, and you are quite sure this feeling will never repeat. A man in black and brown fatigues is in the driver seat of a Lincoln Navigator, it shakes to life on the tarmac as he points at you through gullwing doors.

"Wouldn't you know it, keys were just sitting there dangling. Triton is a little upset with you."

The man taps away at the screen. You ease into a plush leather seat split into four sections—massaging neck, lumbar, and kidney—while the heated seat wraps you in a warmth that slowly erodes your edge, although the chip on your shoulder is stubborn as you make a mental inventory of the falsehoods of Peter Triton, anticipating an argument.

The horizon offers the faintest hint of dawn as you take the 101 north of the airport. Again, a calm happiness is impossible to ignore as such a smooth SFO exit will never occur again. At the 101 overpass where Bayshore Blvd becomes 3rd St a kindly undetonated double tanker stretches across the freeway, leaving only enough width for one vehicle to pass, as you proceed through the eye of the needle.

Ninety-seven feet in the black red sky the Goddess of Victory raises her trident and clutches her wreath, soldiers pose in the plaza of Union Square, taking landscape video of a tank body spinning in place, the targeting software steadies a motionless turret towards the Dewey Monument.

"No one touches Golden Gate Park, I met my first wife there."

Fat cats, escorts, and wealthy retired couples rub sleep from eye, rustled from California king springs, cotton mouthed and barefoot on cold marble, investigating unknown racket, about to be greeted by a welcoming party of Bradley fighting vehicles rumbling through the Financial District.

The serenity of Telegraph Hill is unbroken as six snipers silently sway in the cold morning gusts, Barrett 82A1 .50 caliber rifles sweep three hundred sixty degrees, as the curved blue black arch feeds into crimson tangelo, the grand city beautifully enveloped in color below the two hundred ten foot vantage atop Coit Tower.

An Abrams' crunchy crawl across crumpling sheet metal reflects off the edifice of the Pier 29 Bulkhead Building, smashing over and through Pier 27 parking, brushing aside the chain link fencing to put San Francisco Bay on 120 mm overwatch, while the tank driver debates whether Allstate and Geico cover coups d'état.

13

The crushed quartz façade of the Transamerica Pyramid towers eight hundred fifty-three feet. Eighteen elevators, but only two head to the top, their shafts creating wings below the triangular tower above the forty-eighth floor. Peter Triton appraises his territory. Coasting at Clay and Sansome, the transparent gullwing canopy of the Lincoln reveals a suspended, spinning M777 Howitzer, drawn skyward by the massive construction crane secured to the roof of a neighboring skyscraper.

Parking the vehicle in the intersection of Clay and Montgomery, your driver exits after swiping the storage release command. Leaning into the trunk he surfaces with Light Machine Gun resting on his hip, plopping a bipod on the hood of the Lincoln, an M249 SAW is now pointing north on Montgomery. He gestures towards the pyramid.

A matte black Aventador is resting all twelve of its cylinders underneath the crisscrossing concrete design that forms the base of the pyramid. Two dozen armed men and women parade the grounds while shadows playfully dance, a second dangling Howitzer flickering in the morning sun.

Surrounded by four smokey topaz walls you cock your head to an uncanny light jazz instrumental of Dr. Dre's *Some L.A. Niggaz*. The elevator doors open to generic beige hallways with white baseboard molding, the climate controlled air perceptibly lacking oxygen: the casket of corporate America.

The hustle bustle of the conference room increases in volume as you discover it swallows the majority of the square footage on this floor. Peter Triton is wearing no tie with a couture black silk suit by the late Jack Taylor, screaming into a handset. The conference room is pungent with cigar smoke, tinted tempered glass clouding the glare on a breathtaking view of Alcatraz, the dramatic diagonal cut of Columbus Ave, and the Golden Gate.

A California condor, no, an AH-64 Apache slowly travels the silent, graceful line in the atmosphere beyond the windows. The bow of a Ticonderoga class warship peeks from below the Golden Gate Bridge, one mile northwest of the St. Francis Yacht Club.

Five older men sit in the southwest corner of the room, legs crossed and smoking Cohiba Behike cigars, drinking Balvenie 50, wearing smoked lenses and dressed immaculately in black suits like five versions of Karl Lagerfeld circa 1984.

"Toffee, honey, oak, and nearly the combined age of the three nocturnal creatures Edgar will send to my penthouse this evening."

Laughter fills the room as Mallory momentarily divides the pack and pours two snorts into a pair of Glencairn whiskey glasses. She is moving towards you in the high fashion version of an oversized shirt and loose denim, two levels of khaki and both overmatched at concealing her curvature.

"Yes, damn it, eighteen million for what? Get it up here now. Pike, listen, no aircraft anywhere near that ship. The only thing they're getting from us is a MARTE MK2/S. I want every tank turret and every piece of artillery tracking that sack of dust, just in case."

Holding the crystal in your palm, drinking liquid gold, watching the dots move below. Civilians have braved the new day, traffic control is successfully in execution. Columbus Ave is beginning to populate. Mallory is watching at the window beside you, her face warmed by the light from a prism of tinted glass.

"You! I could really use a thermobaric weapon right now!"

Triton is pointing and thrusting his arm rapidly towards the window with an unintentionally comical whistling of silk fabric.

"If non-violence leads to the highest ethics, where does a twenty-two thousand pound bomb take us? The unalienable right to shock and awe, what constitutional principle are you returning?"

"Leverage! LE-VER-AGE!"

The five men sit silently, watching.

"I see through you, Simon."

Triton's jaw clenches as his eyes open wide, speaking with sclera. A low, rough croak from the radio cuts the tense moment.

"You slipped up, son. You slipped up."

The voice is gravelly gruff, a flat hoarse tone of an esophagus that has smoked many a Marlboro. Down the boardroom table, and through the glass, a massive Ticonderoga class warship is slowly progressing eastward at the heart of the San Francisco Bay.

"I think you might have punched your own ticket."

The gentlemen polish off the bottle as they spread around one more round. One uncricks his neck and extends his arm across the back of an empty office chair, sporting the smirk of intrigued anticipation. Triton storms across the room and clutches the radio handset.

"I am sixty-seven God damn years old, ain't got no daddy, son! Ooh, you found your way onto our frequency, you Navy boys can really cut a rug. I thought all you San Diego sissies had the Baja sniffles. What are you doing out of quarantine? Identify yourself!"

"Commander Caesar Narwen."

Triton's silver hair is falling over his ears, his beet red face looking around the room in confused mockery.

"I will say, old sport, I'll figure out how you got up here so fast. I'll find your mole, slit his throat, and send him out on a Viking funeral right up to your little tugboat there. Speaking of which, where is your escort fleet? Did you get permission from mommy and daddy to be out here, Caesarino?"

"Think of me as the cannibalistic embryo in the stomach of the mother tiger shark."

"Wow. Well, you enjoy your little pleasure cruise because I'm going to send you something to snack on real soon."

"Triton, you're standing next to a boardroom table inside a conference room, and I'm standing next to an Aegis Combat System inside a Ticonderoga class guided missile cruiser."

"You have any additional factoids, Commander? I've got the morning news in fifteen minutes and then I'm going to talk to your boss and get your ass fired."

Narwen's lip smacking is audible as if he is preparing something. An even lower, slightly accented voice returns.

"I don't deal with psychos. I put 'em away."

Triton tosses the handset against the equipment and holds up his palms, puffing air from his lower lip to blow hair from his eyes, looking at his watch, mumbling to himself.

"Tell me I can't, how much time does it take, helicopter fuel, sink that battleship."

Triton reaches back to the radio but thinks twice, realizing Narwen is listening in. He points at you as if he's stoking another argument. Mallory slicks her hair back.

"This is insane. I need a cigarette. There is a sandwich shop down the street that makes the best turkey, cranberry, cream cheese sandwich you will ever taste. Let's go see if any of the employees came to work this morning."

Triton stands up straight and grabs both of his lapels, adjusting his jacket.

"Get me two."

Once again enclosed in smokey topaz your eyes are on Mallory as the doors thump closed. She presses the back of her skull into the wall, eyes closed, face upwards. Wagner's *Das Rheingold - Vorspiel* builds, the magical notes climbing as you descend. No words are spoken. The elevator rings its electronic bell and the doors open to a stunning blonde and six frazzled underlings. Heather McPhee and the Channel Four News Team attempt to board the elevator, stepping back when they realize you and Mallory need to exit first. McPhee shoots a catty look in the direction of you and Mallory. Mallory curls back a sharp toothed grin and nods to McPhee, angling her body to slip through the news team. The lobby is littered with the newspapermen that still write newspapers, media pundits, gossip gurus, social media influencers, and local news reporters, all in some stage of security frisk. You follow Mallory through the exit.

"Lazaro Brothers. I'm going to find a cigarette. I'll meet you at the restaurant."

She puts her manicured hands on your shoulders, nodding, brushes a stray hair from your forehead, and laughs as she turns to strut Washington Ave like a catwalk. You turn south and walk down Montgomery St—by the unopened Wells Fargo History Museum, with its gold dust and stagecoach— until you reach a charming delicatessen with Lazaro Bros. in red and green signage, and wave after wave of howling guitar escaping through the open windows.

Inside two men are donning aprons and engaged in horseplay behind the counter. Three screens display the Jimi Hendrix Experience finishing up their set at the 1967 Monterey Pop Festival, one screen has the Channel Four morning news on mute.

"Are you the Lazaro brothers?"

"Nah, fool, we're the Rodriguez brothers. We're the only ones who live in the city. The Lazaros live in Marin. Happy New Year! No reglas, baby," exclaims the man as he points to the hand cannon strapped to your chest.

"Not exactly. I hear you can't miss the turkey, cranberry, cream cheese. Four, please."

"You heard right. No problem, just give us a few minutes, there are only two of us today… but rejoice in the fact that all of today's profits go directly to the worker! Aye!"

One of los hermanos Rodriguez sprays the other with a squeeze bottle of mayonnaise before he can finish his speech. The giggling crescendos as Jimi Hendrix lays down his guitar, leaning from his knees to kiss it goodbye, throwing the match that sets the blaze, fingers wiggling and beckoning, grabbing it by the neck, swinging it over his head and reducing it to flaming pieces against the stage.

Turkey, cranberry, and cream cheese sandwiches cost money. You realize you're not carrying money, just seven hollow points and a butterfly blade, the breath in your lungs, the blood through your heart, and a phantom bitcoin wallet. You'll figure it out. A world of possibilities as long as you live.

"Clean up your Hendrix, dog. This is what's up."

Three screens cut to Jimi with the red headband, white tassels flowing as he grins through his trip, swaying and manipulating the upside down Fender like no other. The fourth screen displays a fifteen second bumper promoting the upcoming segment with Triton. He and Heather McPhee are standing at the pyramid windows, overlooking the bay, smiling, as text crawls the bottom of the screen displaying social media's reaction to everything from Triton's choice in suiting to the paramilitary occupation of San Francisco.

There are advertisements for opioid induced constipation medication, reverse mortgages, ultra-high interest credit cards, and a beer brand owned by Brazilians, operated by Belgians, and marketed as America. Hendrix absorbs the eagerness of the crowd as he adjusts tuning, slipping into the first six notes of *Star Spangled Banner.*

The fourth screen fades-in to Heather McPhee explaining something into her microphone. Jimi Hendrix unleashes the wailing, distorted, finger tapping anthem like it was falling down the stairs in slow motion. Triton's face fills most of the screen and you can see him mouth "ladies and gentlemen." You're waving to one of the Rodriguez brothers to unmute the newscast, but they are too firmly entrenched in sandwich construction. The whammy bar wobbles the notes as you see a smoke signal puff from the deck of the Ticonderoga, so deep in the zoomed distance behind Triton's head.

A loud cough in the sky, you run to the doorframe and look towards the bay. Screaming in the troposphere is a freshly ignited Tomahawk missile, wings unfolded for lift, air scoop exposed and turbofan jet engine rocketing south at five hundred fifty miles per hour.

You watch the shooting star travel four miles in twenty-three seconds. Buzzing Alcatraz on flyby, soaring over Fisherman's Wharf as the Fender screams, across Columbus Ave and Broadway, be it ever where freemen shall stand. Time stops as the explosion rips the top three floors into an unknown dimension of fire, the triangular tower suspended in flame like the Eye of Providence. The concussive force knocks you off balance. An elongated fireball erupts towards the south. The smoldering, detached tower is approaching terminal velocity as it tumbles towards pavement. A lake of fire flowing from the beheaded building ejects flame and blackness.

Tempered glass hangs in the air like stardust, the sun's light golden through the smoke. Glittering, captivating your mind: the shimmering ocean west of the path, smiling dimes to the north, unachieved harmony, the pendulum's prospects of positivity. Serendipity. Who are you, what do your hands produce? They deserve goodness. Howitzer shells and Hellfire missiles answer the call of the Tomahawk with exponentially thunderous force, yet the only sound reverberating in your skull is the deafening echo of three words:

Do. You. Believe

Zack Roberts is a product of Southern California.

He attended Loyola High School of Los Angeles, Santa Monica College, and holds a Bachelor of Arts in psychology from the University of California, San Diego.

California 2020 is his debut novel.

www.livershotpublishing.com/zacharyroberts